THE MAN OF FEELING

HENRY MACKENZIE was born in Edinburgh on 6 August 1745. The son of a doctor, he was educated at Edinburgh High School and the University. After a legal apprenticeship with George Inglis of Redhall he was admitted Attorney in the Court of Exchequer in Scotland in 1765. He worked at the London Exchequer until 1769, when he returned to Edinburgh and set up his own practice in the Court of Exchequer. From 1771 he became a leading taxation attorney, frequently visiting London, where he got to know many of the prominent legal and political figures of the day. *The Man of Feeling* was published in 1771 by the London publisher T. Cadell and was an immediate success; it sold out in under two months and had reached its sixth edition by 1791. Mackenzie published two other novels: *The Man of the World* (1773) and *Julia de Roubigné* (1777), and also a successful play, *The Prince of Tunis* (1773). He married Penuel Grant, daughter of the baronet who was chief of that clan, in 1776. They had eleven children. In 1777 he joined the Mirror Club, an Edinburgh literary society, editing their journals *The Mirror* (1779–80) and *The Lounger* (1785–7). Mackenzie wrote stories for both journals, while his review of Robert Burns's poems in *The Lounger* no. 97, calling him 'this heaven-taught ploughman', was the first important criticism of the poet. A leading member of Edinburgh's literary society, Mackenzie was also a founder member of the Royal Society of Edinburgh (1783) and helped form the Highland Society of Scotland (1784). During the politically troubled decade of the 1790s he wrote political pamphlets for the Pitt government. In 1804 he chaired a committee on the authenticity of the Ossian poems 'translated' by James Macpherson. From 1799 until his death on 14 January 1835 Mackenzie was Comptroller of Taxes for Scotland.

BRIAN VICKERS has been Professor of English Literature and Director of the Centre for Renaissance Studies at ETH Zurich since 1975. He has written extensively on Bacon, on Renaissance science and technology, and on classical rhetoric. He has edited *Francis Bacon* for the Oxford Authors series, and Bacon's *Essays* for Oxford World's Classics.

STEPHEN BENDING and STEPHEN BYGRAVE both teach in the Department of English at the University of Southampton.

OXFORD WORLD'S CLASSICS

*For over 100 years Oxford World's Classics have brought
readers closer to the world's great literature. Now with over 700
titles—from the 4,000-year-old myths of Mesopotamia to the
twentieth century's greatest novels—the series makes available
lesser-known as well as celebrated writing.*

*The pocket-sized hardbacks of the early years contained
introductions by Virginia Woolf, T. S. Eliot, Graham Greene,
and other literary figures which enriched the experience of reading.
Today the series is recognized for its fine scholarship and
reliability in texts that span world literature, drama and poetry,
religion, philosophy and politics. Each edition includes perceptive
commentary and essential background information to meet the
changing needs of readers.*

OXFORD WORLD'S CLASSICS

═══

HENRY MACKENZIE

The Man of Feeling

═══

Edited by
BRIAN VICKERS

With an Introduction and Notes by
STEPHEN BENDING *and* STEPHEN BYGRAVE

OXFORD
UNIVERSITY PRESS

OXFORD
UNIVERSITY PRESS

Great Clarendon Street, Oxford OX2 6DP

Oxford University Press is a department of the University of Oxford.
It furthers the University's objective of excellence in research, scholarship,
and education by publishing worldwide in

Oxford New York

Athens Auckland Bangkok Bogotá Buenos Aires Cape Town
Chennai Dar es Salaam Delhi Florence Hong Kong Istanbul Karachi
Kolkata Kuala Lumpur Madrid Melbourne Mexico City Mumbai Nairobi
Paris São Paulo Shanghai Singapore Taipei Tokyo Toronto Warsaw

with associated companies in Berlin Ibadan

Oxford is a registered trade mark of Oxford University Press
in the UK and in certain other countries

Published in the United States
by Oxford University Press Inc., New York

Note on the Text © Brian Vickers 1987
Introduction, Select Bibliography, Chronology, Appendices, Explanatory Notes
© Stephen Bending and Stephen Bygrave 2001

British Library Cataloguing in Publication Data

Data available

Library of Congress Cataloging in Publication Data

Data available

ISBN-13: 978-0-19-284032-5
ISBN-10: 0-19-284032-0

4

Typeset in Ehrhardt
by RefineCatch Limited, Bungay, Suffolk
Printed in Great Britain by
Clays Ltd, St Ives plc

CONTENTS

INTRODUCTION

Following a trail in search of something which is not there, Henry Mackenzie's *The Man of Feeling* begins at a 'false point'. From the first, Mackenzie disrupts the conventions of narrative order, offering us a story which starts nowhere in particular and concludes with only the most ambiguous of morals. Indeed, while on the opening page the sporting curate accepts his disappointment with a sigh that 'all is vanity and vexation of spirit', the fragmentariness of Mackenzie's narrative may leave us far less confident that such conventional morality is an adequate account of human experience.

In the novel Mackenzie traces his hero, Harley, through a series of fragmentary scenes nested within the account of a found manuscript. Each scene seems to demonstrate Harley's benevolence in an apparently uncaring commercial world, and yet that benevolence is always complicated. In scene after scene Harley encounters the feeling body, the body in distress, which incites his sympathetic fine-feeling, but the reader, who witnesses these scenes at a remove, must inevitably also recognize them as reliant on the very suffering they lament. Is there perhaps a pleasure to be found in the suffering of others? Are Harley's spontaneous acts of sympathy selfless acts of charity, or does benevolence simply attempt to mask the economic and social inequalities which privilege the leisured gentleman and his pursuit of pleasure? This uncertainty over the moral nature of human relationships marks out *The Man of Feeling* as a major work of sentimental fiction.

At the start of the novel we learn that the curate has been using its manuscript as wadding for his gun, and as he describes it, it is 'a bundle of little episodes, put together without art, and of no importance on the whole, with something of nature, and little else in them'. Where the text breaks off, the editor's description might well echo the reader's own feelings:

recitals of little adventures, in which the dispositions of a man, sensible to judge, and still more warm to feel, had room to unfold themselves. Some instruction, and some example, I make no doubt they contained; but it is likely that many of those, whom chance has led to a perusal of what I have already presented, may have read it with little pleasure, and will feel no disappointment from the want of those parts which I have been unable to procure. To such as may have expected the intricacies of a novel, a few incidents in a life undistinguished, except by some features of the heart, cannot have afforded much entertainment. (p. 93)

Is it really so artless? If the book is all mediated to us via the editor of a dead man's papers, who is the first-person narrator? Moreover, 'bundles' may have greater significance than the curate imagines: according to the philosopher David Hume, even the self is no more than 'a bundle or collection of different perceptions, which ... are in a perpetual flux and movement'.[1] Mackenzie's text maintains a similar sense of the fragmentary and apparently arbitrary. It starts with Chapter XI and soon moves into a pattern of missing chapters, editorial interventions, and ellipses. Late in the narrative Harley is even abandoned briefly to begin the apparently unconnected tale of Mountford and Sedley (p. 87). The device allows Mackenzie to leave out dull connecting narratives and to offer in their place a series of tales of distress (such as that of old Edwards in Chapter XXIV, first seen as a white-haired old soldier). Such scenes are quintessential to the sentimental novel, where absences and gaps are extended into a failure to speak, and where a marked sense of distance appears between the sentimental hero and the society in which he finds himself.

Sentiment, Sensibility, and the Novel

Janet Todd's introduction to the literature of sensibility (a related term which has only ever been unsatisfactorily distinguished from 'sentiment') begins with sensibility as a discourse in which

[1] *A Treatise of Human Nature*, ed. L. A. Selby-Bigge, 2nd edn., rev. P. H. Nidditch (Oxford: Clarendon Press, 1978), 252 [Book II, Part iv, sec. vi].

the moral and aesthetic are inseparable and which has its own hierarchies, its own formal taxonomies and procedures.[2] The subject-matter of these works would very often be the poor, dogs, idiots, old women, 'primitive' people, or children. Their syntax is characteristically fragmentary, to produce the effect of what Samuel Richardson called 'writing to the moment'. The sentimental novel as a whole tends to be structured episodically or fragmentarily, often featuring tableaux or 'scenes' of those in 'distress' which work in exemplary rather than discursive terms. The spectacle of emotion can take the place of persuasion, arresting or usurping argument. However, the reader of sentimental fiction is implicated in a troublesome sociability of mixed motives and alternative perspectives. Even the claims for the fundamental goodness of human nature are made problematic, as the social world the hero meets is strikingly free from human kindness.

Samuel Johnson's much-quoted remark that one must read Richardson 'for the sentiment, and consider the story as only giving occasion to the sentiment' points to the power of sentimental fiction to engage the reader with a moral and emotional immediacy which is to be distinguished from mere 'plot' or storytelling. In *Clarissa* above all, Richardson provided the model of the heroine as a woman of suffering sensibility whose reward is either death or marriage. From around the middle of the eighteenth century, however, a new fashion emerged in fiction for a man of feeling who also suffers because he is either too good or too foolish for the world. Sarah Fielding—sister of Henry—wrote *David Simple* between 1744 and 1753; Henry Brooke's *The Fool of Quality* appeared between 1764 and 1767 (the French translation of *The Man of Feeling*—as *L'Homme Sensible* (Amsterdam and Paris, 1775)—attributed the novel to Brooke), and Oliver Goldsmith's *The Vicar of Wakefield* was published in 1766, but these were only amongst the best-known examples of what became a flourishing and indeed lucrative genre.

One sign of the widespread popularity of sensibility and of

[2] Janet Todd, *Sensibility: An Introduction* (London: Methuen, 1987).

Mackenzie's account of it in particular appeared in 1777, when 'An Elegiac Ode, to the Memory of the Rev. Charles Stewart Eccles' mistakenly celebrated an Irish clergyman at Bath as the author of *The Man of Feeling*. Eccles had transcribed the whole of the novel, with crossings-out, marginal additions, blots, and so on. The publishers denied his claim to be the author, but this was an understandable scam given the context which this hugely popular novel of 1771 invoked for itself. Not only had it been published anonymously, but its text also purports to reach us via the editor of a dead man's papers (as it does in much Gothic and sentimental fiction, notably in Goethe's *Werther*), as the fragmentary transcript of a sentimental life. Eccles provided his own sentimental coda, in life, if not fiction: he died trying to save a boy from drowning in the River Avon. As the publisher of the poem wrote to Mackenzie: 'Should You, to a Demonstration, make it appear that you are the *Author*—still you must agree with me that in the last Act of Mr. Eccles' Life he proved himself—A Man of Feeling.'[3]

As this episode demonstrates, Mackenzie's novel is explicitly within a mid-eighteenth-century tradition of fiction and philosophical writing which takes as its subject the state of human nature, and sees sentiment and benevolence as fundamental to that state—a tradition which *The Man of Feeling* both exploits and encapsulates. Indeed, sentiment (and sensibility) became vogue terms, especially in the second half of the century, connoting a stress on sympathy and the passions which has important implications for politics and for gender-relations as well as for ways of reading in later texts. In all of these concerns, Mackenzie draws on the developing philosophical discussion of sentiment emerging from what has become known as the Scottish Enlightenment. In the Edinburgh where Mackenzie himself was born and educated, figures such as Adam Ferguson, Francis

[3] *Literature and Literati: The Literary Correspondence and Notebooks of Henry Mackenzie*, Volume 1: *Letters 1766-1827*, ed. Horst W. Drescher, Publications of the Scottish Studies Centre of the Johannes Gutenberg Universität Mainz in Germersheim (Frankfurt am Main: Verlag Peter Lang, 1989), 73-7; see also *Boswell's Life of Johnson*, ed. G. B. Hill, rev. L. F. Powell, 6 vols (Oxford: Clarendon Press, 1934), i. 360.

Hutcheson, David Hume, and Adam Smith, mounted a sustained interrogation of human nature that consistently sought to account for the individual in relation to social institutions, economic structures, and historical conditions. Always near the centre of such discussion was the need to confront the competing accounts of human action as fundamentally selfish or fundamentally benevolent. It is with such debates that sentimental fiction engages.

Philosophically, arguments for 'sentiment' depend upon a conviction that 'reason' alone is limited. We prefer some things to others simply because we are innately predisposed to prefer the good to the bad, the beautiful to the ugly, and so on. Sentiment is this predisposition, and is characteristically a concern of the legal, historical, and anthropological studies of the Scottish Enlightenment, in each case designed to demonstrate that human behaviour may be motivated primarily by impulses of benevolence or sympathy rather than by those of acquisitiveness or mere self-preservation. David Hume, for example, argues that benevolence is not just beautiful but useful as well. It promotes notions of community over the selfish individualistic ethic associated with Bernard Mandeville's *The Fable of the Bees* (1714) or with the new discipline of political economy. Adam Smith—whose work encompasses both these putatively opposed discourses—writes of the amiable or social passions:

There is a helplessness in the character of extreme humanity which more than anything interests our pity. There is nothing in itself which renders it either ungraceful or disagreeable. We only regret that it is unfit for the world, because the world is unworthy of it, and because it must expose the person who is endowed with it as a prey to the perfidy and ingratitude of insinuating falsehood.[4]

The question is whether such a person is superior or inferior to the world for which she or he is unfitted: whether, in the case of

---

[4] Adam Smith, *The Theory of Moral Sentiments* (Indianapolis: Liberty Press, 1976), 96. As G. J. Barker-Benfield comments in quoting this passage from Smith: 'The latter sentence could be the plot of a sentimental novel': *The Culture of Sensibility: Sex and Society in Eighteenth-Century Britain* (Chicago: University of Chicago Press, 1992), 140–1.

The Man of Feeling, Harley is an *idiot savant*, and may even be Christlike, or rather is simply a gullible fool.

In Mackenzie's novel there is only the merest background hint of perspectives other than Harley's own, but we are made insistently aware that 'sentimental' responses of the kind promoted by Rousseau or Hutcheson may be read in very different ways. One such moment comes at the end of Chapter XXVI when, having 'rescued' a prostitute and given her what money he has, Harley is unable to pay his bill in the tavern and leaves his watch as a pledge. The waiter sneers as Harley leaves, and at this point we are moved to ask who is right. The waiter is eventually revealed to be cynical, and Harley in the right, but it is also suggested very early on that Harley's sentimentalism is regarded as quite comically excessive by others. It is said of Miss Walton's voice, for instance: 'The effect it had upon Harley, himself used to paint ridiculously enough; and ascribed it to powers, which few believed, and nobody cared for' (p. 13). Men of Feeling, that is, generally do not represent a social consensus nor an example for others to follow. Harley's eccentricity challenges the reader to fill in the gaps, to unify the fragments (or at least to be attracted by these things), a challenge also signalled in some of the chapter titles ('The Man of Feeling in a Brothel', for example.)

The word 'sentimental' might be broken down into its etymological elements and defined as 'thinking through feeling'. Sentiment has a physical basis. It begins in the body, in the senses. We recognize it by bodily signs: fainting or swooning, crying, an inability to speak. To represent it there is a vocabulary, derived from eighteenth-century physiology and psychology, words such as 'impression', 'sensation', 'nerve', 'fibre', 'vibration', and 'thrill', or more apparently to do with leaving the body behind, with a temporary loss of sensation, such as 'melting', 'swooning', 'transport', and so on. If these tropes describe physical responses, they are often designed, as pornography is, to elicit them.[5]

There is also a kind of democratic potential implied by sentimentalism, in that bodies may seem to be much the same across

[5] See Janet Todd, *Sensibility*.

classes. Sentiment is anti-aristocratic, claiming that there is a meritocracy of feeling, apparently unconnected to birth or wealth. The protagonists (or at least the subjects) of sentimental fiction are often peasants or women. Sentimental fiction addresses a politically disenfranchised audience, largely the urban middle class and women, and it is associated with female readers: one anthology of Mackenzie's writings says of *The Man of Feeling* in particular that 'The fair especially, and the young, were its most passionate admirers'.[6] In fact, the sentimental body is clearly gendered. Men are associated with conceptual mastery, a language of ideas, and with the mind, where women are associated with practical expression and may speak an affective language, a language of the heart.

Such rigid gender and class assumptions may, however, be questioned by the form of the novel. Notably, sentiment can also feminize: bodily rather than rational, and marked by tears, it softens the masculine obduracy of the society in which Harley moves. Civilization was recognized to be the product of wealth and increasing global power, but *The Man of Feeling* takes part in a debate, particularly prominent in the Scottish Enlightenment, over the reciprocal effects of gender and refinement. Literary form could provide a focus for this debate. If the modes of epic and the heroic were no longer tenable, how was masculinity to be represented? In culture at large, to 'civilize' is also to 'feminize', and while this was on the one hand to be welcomed, on the other it ran the risk of leaving those males who constituted civilization effeminate and weak. So there is a paradox, in that while empire relies upon a traditional heroic masculinity, what it produces may be a feminized masculinity no longer capable of sustaining that empire. As G. J. Barker-Benfield has argued, 'popular novels written by men in the 1760s and 1770s were preoccupied with the meanings of sensibility for manhood'[7] and the ambiguity we now tend to read into the novels of Laurence Sterne or Mackenzie reflects this contemporary ambivalence, arising not least from the fact that writers of both sexes clearly had the increasing audience

---

[6] *The Beauties of Mackenzie* (Cupar: R. Tullis, 1813), p. v.
[7] Barker-Benfield, *The Culture of Sensibility*, 142.

of female readers in mind when offering the humane feminized hero.

There are other kinds of masculinity in the sentimental novel besides the feminized variety represented by Harley (there is, for instance, the sensuality rather than sentiment indulged in by the rake or libertine, such as Richardson's Lovelace or the villains of Gothic fiction), but in each case the male protagonist's actions mark him out as separated from the society in which he finds himself. A characteristic aspect of that separation is the tendency to move from narrative action to tableau and still life. One example is the carefully constructed tableau in the debtors' prison:

On something like a bed, lay a man with a face seemingly emaciated with sickness, and a look of patient dejection. A bundle of dirty shreds served him for a pillow, but he had a better support—the arm of a female who kneeled beside him, beautiful as an angel, but with a fading languor in her countenance, *the still life of melancholy, that seemed to borrow its shade from the object on which she gazed.* (p. 90; italics ours)

The protagonist usually pays these painterly scenes he views 'the tribute of some tears' (p. 26) and they usually lead to action, as they do here. However, they are in part also an attempt to move outside or disregard the complexities of the world in which the hero finds himself: divorced from the competing narratives in which it might be placed, the sentimental 'scene' appeals to a sense of interaction and appears to offer a moment of simple human contact between individuals. Such fragmentary narratives lend themselves to free-standing appreciation, and indeed book-sellers often removed them from their original context to be republished in giftbooks and anthologies.[8]

One scene, apparently paradigmatic of sensibility, is also close to farce:

[8] Mackenzie's 'Story of Old Edwards' along with his 'Story of La Roche' from *The Mirror* (the story praised by Scott) are both in George Nicholson (ed.), *Literary Miscellany; or Elegant Selections of the Most Admired Fugitive Pieces* and *Extracts from Works of the Greatest merit* (London, 1793–1803). The 'Story of Old Edwards' (along with an extract from Thomas Day's *Sandford and Merton*) is also in *Moral Tales by Esteemed Writers* (1800).

His daughter was now prostrate at his feet. 'Strike,' said she, 'strike here a wretch, whose misery cannot end but with that death she deserves.' Her hair had fallen on her shoulders! Her look had the horrible calmness of out-breathed despair! Her father would have spoken; his lip quivered, his cheek grew pale! His eyes lost the lightening of their fury! There was a reproach in them, but with a mingling of pity! He turned them up to heaven—then on his daughter.—He laid his left hand on his heart—the sword dropped from his right—he burst into tears. (p. 50)

We are as likely to find this scene comic as affecting. Of course the word 'sentimental' and its cognates these days always has a derogatory sense, a sense of an undesirable and sometimes embarrassing excess of feeling; it links qualities of feeling sorry for yourself, of being conscious of your own woes, with praiseworthy qualities such as a susceptibility to the feelings of others and a responsiveness to beauty. The closeness of the sentimental effect to camp, as here, is also suggested by the Index of Tears included in Victorian editions (reprinted here as Appendix 3).

Indeed the transition from pathos to absurdity seems to have occurred within Mackenzie's lifetime. Reading *The Man of Feeling* at 14 Lady Louisa Stuart 'had a secret dread I should not cry enough to gain the credit of proper sensibility'. In 1826, however, she recorded what happened when a country-house group chose to read the novel aloud:

I, who was the reader, had not seen it for many years. The rest did not know it at all. I am afraid I perceived a sad change in it, or myself, which was worse, and the effect altogether failed. Nobody cried, and at some passages, the touches that I used to think so exquisite—oh dear! They laughed. I thought we never should get over Harley's walking down to breakfast with his shoe-buckles in his hand. Yet I remember so well its first publication, my mother and sisters crying over it, dwelling on it with rapture.[9]

It is noticeable that, whether we laugh or cry, the book elicits a physical response. Indeed, words are usually insufficient: 'There were a thousand sentiments;—but they gushed so impetuously on

[9] Wilfred Partington (ed.), *The Private Letter-Books of Sir Walter Scott* (London: Hodder & Stoughton, 1930), 273.

his heart, that he could not utter a syllable' (p. 78). Feeling is beyond words, and is played out on the body. The physical response does not lie or alter, as words do:

> It ne'er was apparell'd with art,
> On words it could never rely;
> It reign'd in the throb of my heart,
> It gleam'd in the glance of my eye.
>
> (p. 85)

'It escapes discussion—it is only to be felt', as Mary Wollstonecraft's heroine writes in her rhapsody on sensibility in *Mary, or The Wrongs of Woman* (1788).

In his biographical notice of Henry Mackenzie (whom he there calls 'our Northern Addison'), Walter Scott was sure that *The Man of Feeling* represented a phenomenology of feeling; that it was 'rather the history of effects produced on the human mind by a series of events, than the narrative of those events themselves'. As Scott suggests, Mackenzie's book may not be a commentary upon the sentimental effect so much as a sourcebook or repertoire of such effects.

Absence is one of the major tropes of sentimental fiction. A text such as *The Man of Feeling* repeatedly offers us gaps, silences, and inaction or inadequate action in the face of suffering, injustice, and large-scale social ills. What kind of model is this for society? In what sense does such 'benevolence' demonstrate the innate goodness of human nature it claims? Certainly its fragmentariness allows for the obtrusion of political comment—for example, on the squire who has knocked down a school because it interrupted the view and ploughed up the green on which the children played. Characteristically, such an attack may be modified even before we come to read it, as when Harley criticizes British colonization of India under the chapter-title 'The Man of Feeling talks of what he does not understand'. The form allows for the inclusion of politically controversial material, though it is only inconsistently reformist, and in a fragmented text the status of such moments of moral outrage is inevitably uncertain. In Mackenzie's later novel *Julia de Roubigné*, the utopian reform of a Jamaican plantation amounts to little more than an ameliorative vision of slavery. Sentimentalism seems to have limited answers to political problems: Harley's attempts to remove social distress are both curtailed and misunderstood.[10] This absence or limitation of action marks out many sentimental texts. If the modern reader is uncertain of Harley's moral stance, that uncertainty is to be found also in the work of such contemporaries of Mackenzie as Richardson, Sarah Fielding, Goldsmith, and Sterne.

Consumption of sentimental texts such as these paradoxically depends on a self-conscious consumer. On the reunion and reconciliation of a father and daughter in *The Man of Feeling*, the common trope of an inability to speak, of the insufficiency of words, is accompanied by an appeal to an audience:

We would attempt to describe the joy which Harley felt on this occasion, did it not occur to us that one half of the world could not understand it though we did, and the other half will, by this time, have understood it without any description at all. (p. 52)

The trope is familiar in sentimental fiction, and is itself about familiarity. The reunion and reconciliation that has just been narrated produces extreme but nevertheless common feeling. This is a refusal rather than a failure of representation: gesturing towards the insufficiency of words, it is accompanied by the flattering invocation of an audience. A response that cannot be gainsaid because it is involuntary also requires the reader to have been educated to discern that response. So confident can Mackenzie be of a sympathetic effect on at least half the world that he does not need to represent its cause. Earlier, the putative editor who has found Harley's fragmentary tale records that:

I was a good deal affected with some very trifling passages in it; and had the name of Marmontel, or a Richardson, been on the title page— 'tis odds that I should have wept: But

---

[10] For a fascinating account of this issue, see Markman Ellis, *The Politics of Sensibility: Race, Gender and Commerce in the Sentimental Novel* (Cambridge: Cambridge University Press, 1996). The relevant chapter from *Julia de Roubigné* is contained below in Appendix 2.

One is ashamed to be pleased with the works of one knows not whom. (p. 5)

Weeping is a spontaneous activity which is nevertheless attended by notions of propriety or decorum: the editor retains self-consciousness and self-control enough to know the boundaries of such propriety. The novelty of the work for its putative first reader is still to be justified in prior, canonical terms; and there was a redoubled irony for the actual first readers of the novel, who had in their hands an anonymous work.

The commonality of sentimental effects makes the reactions of the spectator crucial. 'Spectator', a visual term rather than the aural 'audience', is Adam Smith's term in his *Theory of Moral Sentiments* for the withdrawn figure able to distinguish mere propriety from virtue; the latter is 'far above what is vulgar and ordinary'. 'Sentiment' and 'sensibility' are not universal or democratic qualities, but qualities of a self-consciously distanced spectator.[11]

That mismatch between the private and the public highlights the distinction between a world of public actions and a private sphere of the self in sentimental fiction. In Harley's reactions to suffering there remains a friction between the articulation of subjective responses and the need to ratify those responses within a broader culture. Perhaps, then, we should not think in terms of the wholly private, of some autistic sense of self, but rather of a subjectivity which inevitably requires an audience. If there is a private world of 'feeling', the sensibility which for Harley is a touchstone of authenticity, that sensibility cannot be wholly divorced from the social world in which it is experienced.

Luxury, Commerce, and Money

Mackenzie worked at the London Exchequer until 1769, having moved from Edinburgh after qualifying as an attorney four years earlier, and so was in London when the last parts of Laurence

---

[11] Smith, *The Theory of Moral Sentiments*, 72 [Part I, sec. I, ch. 5].

Sterne's *Tristram Shandy* were being serially published (1759–67). Walter Scott compares a scene from Sterne's *Tristram Shandy*, in which the tear of the Recording Angel blots Uncle Toby's profane oath from the register of heaven with Mackenzie's tale of La Roche from his periodical *The Mirror*: 'Mackenzie has given us a moral truth, Sterne a beautiful trope.' The clear implication is that the binding of subject and object in Mackenzie's story makes his writing sincere in a way that Sterne's 'irresponsible (and nasty) trifling'—as F. R. Leavis was to call it—is not, and that the former is superior.[12] Sterne's final, posthumously published novel *A Sentimental Journey* has so many similarities to Mackenzie's novel that it might seem like a satire on it, were it not for the inconvenient chronology: *A Sentimental Journey* was published three years before *The Man of Feeling*.[13]

Sterne's narrator is a spectator of sentimental events without becoming the kind of sympathetic spectator who participates in such events. He gives charity mainly to female beggars and, as it were, pays for emotion. The language and 'scenes' of his novel continually exploit (down to the very last sentence, and perhaps beyond) the possibility of double entendre in that discourse. Such an ironic awareness of the basic lust and acquisitiveness of the spectator is not antithetical to but the twin of sentiment, not opposite so much as complementary to it.

Though the narrator of *The Man of Feeling* rejects the priority of 'ideas' in perception, he is sure that Harley is an idealist in the colloquial sense of always seeing the world through rose-tinted

---

[12] *The Great Tradition* (1948; Harmondsworth: Penguin, 1962), 11. It is also noticeable that the 'moral truths' Scott recognizes in Mackenzie are secular: there is an invocation of Providence in *The Man of Feeling* (on p. 73), but the first explicit apostrophe to God comes on p. 76.

[13] Mackenzie wrote to his friend James Elphinston shortly after the publication of *The Man of Feeling*: 'An imitation of Sterne had been early objected to me; yet certain it is, that some parts of *The Man of Feeling*, which bear the strongest resemblance to *The Sentimental Journey*, were written, and even read to some of my friends, before the publication of that ingenious performance. Setting out with this principle, that it was an imitation of Sterne, it was rightly pronounced [by the *Monthly Review*] a lame one; because, in truth, no such imitation was intended' (24 June 1771). *Literature and Literati*, ed. Drescher, 55–7.

glasses (p. 13). There is an example of the way the world is antithetical to the man of feeling at the beginning of Chapter XL, in which Harley learns from his manservant, Peter, that Miss Walton is to be married:

The desire of communicating knowledge or intelligence, is an argument with those that hold that man is naturally a social animal. It is indeed one of the earliest propensities we discover; but it may be doubted whether the pleasure (for pleasure there certainly is) arising from it be not often more selfish than social: for we frequently observe the tidings of Ill communicated as eagerly as the annunciation of Good. Is it that we delight in observing the effects of the stronger passions? For we are all philosophers in this respect; and it is perhaps amongst the spectators at Tyburn that the most genuine are to be found. (p. 79)

The reflection on the benevolence of human society at the beginning of this quotation turns into a reflection on the unpleasantness of its motives; Mackenzie's narrator rehearses the opposing positions of a Hobbes and Mandeville on the one hand and a Rousseau or a Hutcheson on the other. In Mackenzie's hands, as in Sterne's, 'sentiment' may carry with it its own critique. *A Sentimental Journey* undermines any confidence in a clear moral position by constantly shifting its perspectives and revelling in the ambiguity of responses. We are never sure if the narrator of *The Man of Feeling* remains in control of the effects and is holding out on us; and of that at least we are always sure with Sterne.

The self-consciousness of the form, then, need not be disabling, as it allows Mackenzie's novel to ask a series of vital questions: what morality is possible in a complex commercial world? Does trying to maintain it make you a saint or a fool? Is sentiment merely a luxury for the leisured classes? Harley seems to offer us an account of feeling in stark contrast to the world of capitalism and commerce: we repeatedly encounter scenes where he wants to remove distress, to end the suffering of the poor; and yet we can also read this as Harley paying for emotional display. For example, in the scene in the debtors' prison referred to earlier, Harley signs away £2,500 to the stranger. Suffering becomes just another commodity, something to be consumed in a commercial transaction.

There are, though, forms of exchange which, though similar to commercial transactions, are morally superior because apparently uncorrupted by pecuniary motives and by the negative effects of commercial success. The latter are what the eighteenth century lumped together under the term 'luxury'. The mid-eighteenth-century debate on luxury, while rooted in classical thought, springs more directly from late-seventeenth-century arguments that luxury is at least a necessary evil in a commercial trading society because it leads to the circulation of commodities, increased employment, and greater wealth for the nation as a whole.[14] That is, a powerful line of argument defends the social and economic inequalities implied by luxury on the grounds that it increases the well-being of all. Set against that economic laissez-faire was the view that luxury represents the moral decay of the nation, destroying an organic sense of community and upsetting a patrician vision of society.

On this reading, sentiment, associated as we have seen with women, with consumption rather than production, and with leisure rather than labour, can always be tainted by the anxiety that it is itself a luxury item in commodity culture, not only an indulgence which society could ill afford but also of the sort that had undermined the classical empires that were the only analogy for mid-century Britain. Part of what is at stake is a nostalgia for a lost age of perfect (often rural) community. Harley's sentimentality, while it might make him superior to 'the world', certainly tends to put him outside rural society. This allows him to view what he is outside of (to construct it as 'scenes'), but it also means that he cannot recapture the innocence of the pastoral modes that represented it. In the second stanza of his pastoral poem, he writes that his pipe is no longer in tune with the times:

[14] See John Sekora, *Luxury: The Concept in Western Thought from Eden to Smollett* (Baltimore: Johns Hopkins University Press, 1977); Christopher Berry, *The Idea of Luxury: A Conceptual and Historical Investigation* (Cambridge: Cambridge University Press, 1994), esp. ch. 6.

> Erewhile were its notes of accord
>   With the smile of the flow'r-footed muse;
> Ah! why by its master implor'd
>   Shou'd it now the gay carrol refuse?

(p. 85)

(The answer to the rhetorical question is: because it is too late.) Like the youth in Gray's *Elegy*, perhaps the only function Harley can perform within the rural society is that of the village idiot. The world is basically against him, not just because of his excessive sensibility, but because he is in love with someone of a higher social class who is heiress to £4,000 a year. As his aunt says, 'now-a-days, it is money, not birth, that makes people respected; the more shame for the times' (p. 80). There seems a radical charge here, in the implicit resistance both to traditional social hierarchy and to a modern status based on wealth.

The sentimental subject, then, wants to be removed from a world of social difference engendered by monetary difference, and yet relies on charitable benevolence to produce moments of sentimental contact. The very sociability the sentimentalist craves, that circulation in society which brings a pleasurable awareness of the circulation of the blood, is implicitly recognized as itself reliant on the circulation of money. And like money, tears—the classic sentimental display of the body's authentic emotion—become a form of payment.

The need to bridge the gap between aspiration and action, the worlds of feeling and money, the political and the fictional, is the product of a political self-consciousness of which paradox is the formal counterpart. Sentiment is a natural instinct, yet a part of women's nature more than men's, and one that tends to be produced by the lower classes only for consumption by the higher. It is an essential reflex, yet presupposes the position of a spectator who has learned the appropriate response. While it raises the status of women as a model for men, it also makes them into victims of their own bodies and the way in which they are interpreted. If Harley is the victim of an uncaring world, the young woman whom he saves from prostitution is of no interest to a man of feeling unless she is a victim.

Sentiment, as we have seen, is marked as feminine by the way it is played out upon bodies and known by bodily signs, but there is also something of hysteria in the way that the body's loss of control in demonstrating sensibility marks it as a site for interpretation. As John Mullan has noted, with particular reference to medical discourse, the hysterical body is treated as a system of signs, but of signs usually interpreted by men.[15] In fiction, the role of interpreter frequently falls upon the male lover and, as Eliza Haywood's novels earlier in the century demonstrated, the ambivalence of bodily signs marks not only a loss of power but the moment of masculine opportunism. Men of feeling run no such risk, and it is Harley's wealth rather than his 'virtue' which is at stake.

Sentimental fiction has an ambivalent relation to all of these issues. On the one hand it highlights and seeks to sympathize with the suffering poor, the victims of an immoral or amoral free market economy. On the other, the 'pleasure' of sympathy relies upon the suffering it apparently laments. The central question asked by sentimental fiction, then, may be a reflexive one: does it do more than demonstrate that sentimentalism is morally irrelevant?

The form of sentimental fiction (its dashes and ellipses, its fragmentariness) seems to have bothered its eighteenth-century readers less than its modern ones. More important to the eighteenth-century reader of *The Man of Feeling* was its capacity—apparently without irony—to provoke tears, and perhaps too its ability gently to intervene in those adversarial political and social controversies outlined here. This is not to say that Mackenzie's novel can be collapsed, merely into documentary evidence within an account of sentiment or consumerism. The novel resists such collapse partly because its fragmentary and exclamatory form has become strange to modern readers, teasing them— and making them work. *The Man of Feeling*'s appropriation of

---

[15] See John Mullan, *Sentiment and Sociability: The Language of Feeling in the Eighteenth Century* (Oxford: Clarendon Press, 1988).

suffering, its exploitation of visual display, its sentimental scenes, its representation of the eroticized body, and the feminized hero are finally inseparable from its formal exploration of fragments and the non-narrative. Through its form the novel resists becoming part of that very commodity culture which it shows growing into something recognizably like our own. The pleasures of the novel, finally, may lie not in its exemplifying a vanished cultural fashion, but in its examination, and maybe parody, of our own sense of modernity.

NOTE ON THE TEXT

This edition is set up from a copy of the second (corrected) edition of 1771, which was issued in August, and differs from the first edition of April in over four hundred variants. These are undoubtedly the work of Mackenzie himself, and are mainly of a minor nature, offering improvements of style (the *Monthly Review* had criticized the novel's composition, perhaps unfairly: 'it is careless, and abounds in provincial and Scottish idioms'). Grammatical errors and ambiguities (such as an unrelated 'his') are removed, word-order changed (as: 'nauseated listlessness' for 'listless nausea'), frequently to retrieve 'of' from the end of a sentence. Foreign expressions are anglicized ('ceremonial' for '*etiquette*', 'bear-garden' for '*menagerie*') and the punctuation increased (too generously in the number of commas). There are few changes in the more carefully worked passages—the aphoristic endings to sections or the emotionally punctuated sequences—and less changes in the dialogue than in the narrative. Most of the changes are concentrated in little patches, as Mackenzie has rather fussily 'touched up' the style, though not always to its benefit, as a comparison of the two editions will show.

The significant changes are slight: from the literary ancestors of the tale proposed in the introduction (Marmontel, Rousseau, Richardson) the second edition removes Rousseau. The revised edition gives an ironic qualification to this sentence: 'he retired into the country, and made a love-match with a young lady of a temper similar to his own', adding: 'with whom the sagacious world pitied him for finding happiness'. The most important change is the removal of the narrator's comment on the damaged manuscript from between 'Lavinia. A Pastoral' and 'The Pupil. A Fragment' to between 'The Pupil' and Chapter LV—where it makes a better transition to the final episode, though at the cost of a slight inconsistency as now instead of 'two following chapters' there is only one. The third edition (1773) introduces a few alterations in the punctuation (not definitely Mackenzie's) but also some errors.

B.V.

Footnotes in the text are Mackenzie's own; editorial notes are indicated by asterisks.

SELECT BIBLIOGRAPHY

Editions

The Works of Henry Mackenzie, 8 vols. (Edinburgh, 1808), have been reprinted with an introduction by Susan Manning (Routledge/ Thoemmes Press, 1996). Not included in the 1808 *Works* were a paper on dreams and a supplement read to the Royal Society of Edinburgh; Mackenzie's biography of John Home; and some notes towards his Memoirs.

See also:

'Some Account of the Life and Writings of Dr. Blacklock', in Thomas Blacklock, *Poems* (Edinburgh, 1793), pp. i–xxx.

The Anecdotes and Egotisms of Henry Mackenzie, ed. Harold William Thompson (London: Oxford University Press, 1927).

Henry Mackenzie, Letters to Elizabeth Rose of Kilravock: On Literature, Events and People 1768–1815, ed. Horst W. Drescher (Münster: Verlag Aschendorff, 1967), contains an appendix on the books Mackenzie read 1775–81. Elizabeth Rose was his cousin.

Literature and Literati: The Literary Correspondence and Notebooks of Henry Mackenzie, Volume 1: *Letters 1766–1827*, ed. Horst W. Drescher, Publications of the Scottish Studies Centre of the Johannes Gutenberg Universität Mainz in Germersheim (Frankfurt am Main: Verlag Peter Lang, 1989).

Peterson, E. H., 'A Critical Edition of Henry Mackenzie's *Man of Feeling*', unpublished D. Phil. thesis, Oxford University (1990).

Biography

Thompson, Harold William, *A Scottish Man of Feeling* (London, 1931). This remains the standard biography. It includes (pp. 107–11) some earlier letters to Elizabeth Rose.

Critical Studies of Sentiment and Sensibility

Allen, Richard O., 'If You Have Tears: Sentimentalism as Soft Romanticism', *Genre*, 8 (1975), 119–45.

Alexander, David, *Affecting Moments: Prints of English Literature*

Made in the Age of Romantic Sensibility 1775–1800 (York: University of York, 1993).

Armstrong, Nancy, *Desire and Domestic Fiction: A Political History of the Novel* (New York and Oxford: Oxford University Press, 1987).

Barker-Benfield, G. J., *The Culture of Sensibility: Sex and Society in Eighteenth-Century Britain* (Chicago: University of Chicago Press, 1992).

Braudy, Leo, 'The Form of the Sentimental Novel', *Novel*, 7 (Fall 1973), 5–13.

Bredvold, Louis I., *The Natural History of Sensibility* (Detroit: Wayne State University Press, 1962).

Brissenden, R. F., *Virtue in Distress: Studies in the Novel of Sentiment from Richardson to Sade* (London: Hutchinson, 1974).

Brown, Marshall, *Preromanticism* (Stanford: Stanford University Press, 1991).

Campbell, Colin, *The Romantic Ethic and the Spirit of Modern Consumerism* (Oxford: Blackwell, 1987).

Conger, Syndy McMillen (ed.), *Sensibility in Transformation: Creative Resistance to Sentiment from the Augustans to the Romantics* (London and Toronto: Associated University Presses, 1990).

Crane, R. S., 'Studies Toward a Genealogy of the "Man of Feeling"', *ELH* 1 (1934), 205–30.

Eagleton, Terry, *The Rape of Clarissa* (Oxford: Oxford University Press, 1982).

Ellis, Markman, *The Politics of Sensibility: Race, Gender and Commerce in the Sentimental Novel* (Cambridge: Cambridge University Press, 1996).

Foster, James R., *History of the Pre-Romantic Novel in England*, Modern Language Association of America Monograph Series, 17 (New York, 1966; first published 1949).

Friedman, Arthur, 'Aspects of Sentimentalism in Eighteenth-Century Literature', in H. K. Miller *et al.* (eds.) *The Augustan Milieu: Essays Presented to Louis A. Landa* (Oxford: Clarendon Press, 1970).

Greene, Donald 'Latitudarianism and Sensibility: The Genealogy of the "Man of Feeling" Reconsidered', *Modern Philology* 75 (1977), 159–83.

Hagstrum, Jean H., *Sex and Sensibility: Ideal and Erotic Love from Milton to Mozart* (Chicago: University of Chicago Press, 1980).

McGann, Jerome J., *The Poetics of Sensibility: A Revolution in Literary Style* (Oxford: Clarendon Press, 1996).

Markley, Robert, 'Sentimentality as Performance: Shaftesbury, Sterne, and the Theatrics of Virtue', in Felicity Nussbaum and Laura Brown (eds.), *The New Eighteenth Century* (New York: Methuen, 1987), 210–30.

Novak, Maximillian and Anne Mellor (eds.), *Passionate Encounters in a Time of Sensibility* (Cranbury: University of Delaware Press, 1999).

Mullan, John, *Sentiment and Sociability: The Language of Feeling in the Eighteenth Century* (Oxford: Clarendon Press, 1988).

Starr, G. A., 'Only a Boy: Notes on Sentimental Novels', *Genre* (Winter 1977), 501–27.

Todd, Janet, *Sensibility: An Introduction* (London: Methuen, 1987).

—— *The Sign of Angellica: Women, Writing and Fiction, 1660–1800* (London: Virago, 1989), esp. ch. 9, 'Novelists of Sentiment', 161–75.

Van Sant, Ann Jessie, *Eighteenth-Century Sensibility and the Novel: The Senses in Social Context*, Cambridge Studies in Eighteenth-Century English Literature and Thought (Cambridge: Cambridge University Press, 1993).

Critical Studies of Mackenzie and The Man of Feeling

Burling, William J., 'A "Sickly Sort of Refinement": The Problem of Sentimentalism in Mackenzie's *The Man of Feeling*', *Studies in Scottish Literature*, 23 (1988), 136–49.

Burnham, R. Peter, 'The Social Ethos of Mackenzie's *The Man of Feeling*', *Studies in Scottish Literature*, 18 (1983), 123–37.

Cope, Kevin L., 'Defoe, Berkeley, and Mackenzie and the Social Contract of Genre', *Studies on Voltaire and the Eighteenth Century*, 264 (1989), 937–40.

Dwyer, John, 'Clio and Ethics: Practical Morality in Enlightened Scotland', *The Eighteenth Century: Theory and Interpretation*, 30:1 (Spring 1989), 45–72.

Graham, Henry Grey, *Scottish Men of Letters in the Eighteenth Century* (London, 1901).

Harkin, Maureen, 'Mackenzie's Man of Feeling: Embalming Sensibility', *ELH* 61:2 (Summer 1994), 317–40.

Hunt, Leigh, *Classic Tales Serious and Lively: With Critical Essays on the Merits and Reputation of the Authors*, 5 vols. (London, 1807), vol. 1.

London, April, *Women and Property in the Eighteenth-Century English Novel* (Cambridge: Cambridge University Press, 1999), 67–86.

Platzer, Robert, 'Mackenzie's Martyrs: The Man of Feeling as Saintly Fool', *Novel*, 10 (1976), 59–64.

Scott, Walter, 'Mackenzie', in Iaon Williams (ed.), *Sir Walter Scott on Novelists and Fiction* (London: Routledge and Kegan Paul, 1968).

Starr, G. A., 'Sentimental De-education', in Douglas Lane Patey and Timothy Keegan (eds.), *Augustan Studies: Essays in Honour of Irvin Ehrenpreis* (Newark: University of Delaware Press, 1985), 253–62.

—— 'Sentimental Novels of the Later Eighteenth Century', in John Richetti *et al.* (eds.), *The Columbia History of the British Novel* (New York: Columbia University Press, 1994), 181–98.

Suhnel, Rudolf, 'A Plea for *The Man of Feeling*: Henry Mackenzie's Minor Classic in Context, in Wolfgang Adam (ed.), *Das achtzehnte Jahrhundert: Facetten einer Epoche* (Heidelberg: Carl Winter, 1988), 181–7.

Ware, Elaine 'Charitable Actions Re-evaluated in the Novels of Henry Mackenzie', *Studies in Scottish Literature*, 22 (1987), 132–41.

Zimmerman, Everett, 'Fragments of History and *The Man of Feeling*: From Richard Bentley to Walter Scott', *Eighteenth-Century Studies*, 23:3 (Spring 1990), 283–300.

Further Reading in Oxford World's Classics

Austen, Jane, *Sense and Sensibility*, ed. James Kinsley.

Burney, Fanny, *Evelina*, ed. Edward A. Bloom.

Fielding, Henry, *Tom Jones*, ed. John Bender and Simon Stern.

Goldsmith, Oliver, *The Vicar of Wakefield*, ed. Arthur Friedman.

Rousseau, Jean-Jacques, *Confessions*, trans. Angela Scholar, ed. Patrick Coleman.

Scott, Walter, *Waverley*, ed. Claire Lamont.

Sterne, Laurence, *A Sentimental Journey*, ed. Ian Jack.

—— *The Life and Opinions of Tristram Shandy, Gentleman*, ed. Ian Campbell Ross.

A CHRONOLOGY OF HENRY MACKENZIE

1745 Born in Edinburgh (6 August), son of a well-to-do doctor; Jacobite rebellion led by Prince Charles Edward Stuart, defeated by April 1746.

1747 Samuel Richardson's *Clarissa* published between 1 December 1747 and 6 December 1748.

1749 Henry Fielding's *Tom Jones* published.

1751 Mackenzie enters Edinburgh High School; David Hume's *Enquiry Concerning the Principles of Morals* published.

1758 Mackenzie enters Edinburgh University; Hume's *Enquiry Concerning Human Understanding* published; Alexander Gerard's *Essay on Taste* and Adam Smith's *Theory of Moral Sentiments* published the following year.

1760 Laurence Sterne's *Tristram Shandy* (–1767), and James Macpherson's *Fragments of Ancient Poetry* (the 'Ossian' poems) published.

1761 (18 November) Mackenzie articled as clerk to Mr George Inglis, King's Attorney in Exchequer; Jean-Jacques Rousseau's *Nouvelle Héloise* published.

1763 Mackenzie's first publication, a poem in the *Scots Magazine*; Macpherson's *Temora* and Hugh Blair's *On the Poems of Ossian* published.

1764 Ballad of *Duncan* published in the *Scots Magazine*.

1765 After a legal apprenticeship with George Inglis of Redhall, Mackenzie is admitted Attorney in the Court of Exchequer (4 November); proceeds to London for further study of law.

1766 Oliver Goldsmith's *Vicar of Wakefield* published.

1767 *The Man of Feeling* begun in London.

1768 Mackenzie returns to Edinburgh; first mention of *The Man of Feeling* in his correspondence; Sterne's *Sentimental Journey* published.

1771 *The Man of Feeling* published in April, sold out by 1 June; *The Pursuits of Happiness*, a satirical–sentimental poem (influenced by Goldsmith's *Deserted Village*, 1770) published in May; second edition of *The Man of Feeling* published in August; Tobias Smollett's *Humphry Clinker* and James Beattie's *The Minstrel* published.

1773 Mackenzie's *The Man of the World* published in February, and his tragedy *The Prince of Tunis* first performed in March.

1774 Goethe's *Die Leiden des jungen Werthers* (*The Sorrows of Young Werther*) published.

1776 Mackenzie marries Penuel Grant, daughter of the baronet who was chief of that clan, on 6 January (they were to have eleven children); Smith's *Wealth of Nations* published.

1777 Mackenzie joins the Mirror Club, the Edinburgh literary society; his novel *Julia de Roubigné* published.

1779 23 January, *The Mirror* begins publication (ends 27 May 1780).

1783 Mackenzie a founder member of the Royal Society of Edinburgh.

1784 Helps form the Highland Society of Scotland; his *The Ship-wreck* (adapted from George Lillo's *Fatal Curiosity*, 1736) acted in London.

1785 5 February *The Lounger* begins publication (ends 6 January 1787); James Boswell's *Journal of a Tour of the Hebrides* published.

1786 Robert Burns's *Poems in the Scottish Dialect* published: no. 97 of *The Lounger* (9 December) contains Mackenzie's 'Extraordinary Account of Robert Burns, the Ayrshire ploughman', a review of the Kilmarnock Edition of Burns's poems, calling him 'this heaven-taught ploughman'; the review helps to secure Burns's reputation, and perhaps helps to explain the poet's devotion to *The Man of Feeling* (he called the novel 'a book I prize next to the Bible', and is said to have worn out two copies).

1790 Mackenzie's *Letters of Brutus* begun (published in collected form 1791–3); writing political pamphlets for the Pitt government under the patronage of Henry Dundas (later Earl of Melville), though he only claimed authorship of one: *Review of the Principal Proceedings of the Parliament of 1784*, written in 1791–2 and revised by Pitt himself.

1799 Made Comptroller of Taxes for Scotland.

1804 Chairs an inconclusive committee on the authenticity of the Ossian poems, Macpherson's highly successful combination of modern sentiment and ancient epic, which he claimed to have 'translated' from original manuscripts.

1808 Mackenzie's *Works* (8 volumes), supervised by the author; increasing friendship with Walter Scott.

1809 Mackenzie and Scott become directors of the Edinburgh Theatre.

1814 Scott dedicates *Waverley* to Mackenzie.

1822 *Life and Writings of John Home* published.

1824 *Anecdotes and Egotisms* begun.

1831 Dies, 14 January.

THE MAN OF FEELING

INTRODUCTION

M Y dog had made a point on a piece of fallow-ground,* and led the curate and me two or three hundred yards over that and some stubble adjoining, in a breathless state of expectation, on a burning first of September.

It was a false point, and our labour was vain: yet, to do Rover justice, (for he's an excellent dog, though I have lost his pedigree) the fault was none of his, the birds were gone; the curate shewed me the spot where they had lain basking, at the root of an old hedge.

I stopped and cried Hem! The curate is fatter than I; he wiped the sweat from his brow.

There is no state where one is apter to pause and look round one, than after such a disappointment. It is even so in life. When we have been hurrying on, impelled by some warm wish or other, looking neither to the right hand nor to the left—we find of a sudden that all our gay hopes are flown; and the only slender consolation that some friend can give us, is to point where they were once to be found. And lo! if we are not of that combustible race, who will rather beat their heads in spite, than wipe their brows with the curate, we look round and say, with the nauseated listlesness of the king of Israel, 'All is vanity and vexation of spirit.'*

I looked round with some such grave apothegm in my mind, when I discovered, for the first time, a venerable pile, to which the inclosure belonged.* An air of melancholy hung about it. There was a languid stillness in the day, and a single crow, that perched on an old tree by the side of the gate, seemed to delight in the echo of its own croaking.

I leaned on my gun and looked; but I had not breath enough to ask the curate a question. I observed carving on the bark of some of the trees: 'twas indeed the only mark of human art about the place, except that some branches appeared to have been lopped, to give a view of the cascade,* which was formed by a little rill at some distance.

Just at that instant I saw pass between the trees, a young lady with a book in her hand. I stood upon a stone to observe her; but the curate sat him down on the grass, and leaning his back where I stood, told me, 'That was the daughter of a neighbouring gentleman of the name of WALTON, whom he had seen walking there more than once.

'Some time ago,' said he, 'one HARLEY lived there, a whimsical sort of a man I am told, but I was not then in the cure; though, if I had a turn for those things, I might know a good deal of his history, for the greatest part of it is still in my possession.'

'His history!'* said I. 'Nay, you may call it what you please,' said the curate; 'for indeed it is no more a history than it is a sermon. The way I came by it was this: Some time ago, a grave, oddish kind of a man, boarded at a farmer's in this parish: The country people called him The Ghost; and he was known by the slouch in his gait, and the length of his stride. I was but little acquainted with him, for he never frequented any of the clubs here-abouts. Yet for all he used to walk a-nights, he was as gentle as a lamb at times; for I have seen him playing at te-totum* with the children, on the great stone at the door of our church-yard.

'Soon after I was made curate, he left the parish, and went no body knows whither; and in his room was found a bundle of papers, which was brought to me by his landlord. I began to read them, but I soon grew weary of the task; for, besides that the hand is intolerably bad, I could never find the author in one strain for two chapters together: and I don't believe there's a single syllogism from beginning to end.'

'I should be glad to see this medley,'* said I. 'You shall see it now,' answered the curate, 'for I always take it along with me a-shooting.' 'How came it so torn?' ''Tis excellent wadding,' said the curate. — This was a plea of expediency I was not in condition to answer; for I had actually in my pocket great part of an edition of one of the German Illustrissimi,* for the very same purpose. We exchanged books; and by that means (for the curate was a strenuous logician) we probably saved both.

When I returned to town, I had leisure to peruse the acquisition I had made: I found it a bundle of little episodes, put together without art, and of no importance on the whole, with something of nature, and little else in them. I was a good deal affected with some very trifling passages in it; and had the name of a Marmontel, or a Richardson,* been on the title-page——'tis odds that I should have wept: But

One is ashamed to be pleased with the works of one knows not whom.

viz pride has a great deal to do w/ enjoyable reading, esp. in the Learned

THE MAN OF FEELING

CHAPTER XI[1]

OF BASHFULNESS—A CHARACTER—HIS OPINION
ON THAT SUBJECT

THERE is some rust about every man at the beginning; though in some nations (among the French, for instance) the ideas of the inhabitants from climate, or what other cause you will, are so vivacious, so eternally on the wing, that they must, even in small societies, have a frequent collision; the rust therefore will wear off sooner: but in Britain, it often goes with a man to his grave; nay, he dares not even pen a *hic jacet** to speak out for him after his death.

'Let them rub it off by travel,' said the baronet's brother, who was a striking instance of excellent metal, shamefully rusted. I had drawn my chair near his. Let me paint the honest old man: 'tis but one passing sentence to preserve his image in my mind.

He sat in his usual attitude, with his elbow rested on his knee, and his fingers pressed on his cheek. His face was shaded by his hand; yet it was a face that might once have been well accounted handsome; its features were manly and striking, and a certain dignity resided on his eyebrows, which were the largest I remember to have seen. His person was tall and well-made; but the indolence of his nature had now inclined it to corpulency.

His remarks were few, and made only to his familiar friends; but they were such as the world might have heard with veneration: and his heart, uncorrupted by its ways, was ever warm in the cause of virtue and his friends.

He is now forgotten and gone! The last time I was at Silton

---

[1] The Reader will remember, that the Editor is accountable only for scattered chapters, and fragments of chapters; the curate must answer for the rest. The number at the top, when the chapter was entire, he has given as it originally stood, with the title which its author had affixed to it.

hall, I saw his chair stand in its corner by the fire-side; there was an additional cushion on it, and it was occupied by my young lady's favourite lap-dog. I drew near unperceived, and pinched its ear in the bitterness of my soul; the creature howled, and ran to its mistress. She did not suspect the author of its misfortune, but she bewailed it in the most pathetic terms; and kissing its lips, laid it gently on her lap, and covered it with a cambric handkerchief. I sat in my old friend's seat; I heard the roar of mirth and gaiety around me: poor Ben Silton! I gave thee a tear then: accept of one cordial drop that falls to thy memory now.

'They should wear it off by travel.' '—Why, it is true,' said I, 'that will go far; but then it will often happen, that in the velocity of a modern tour, and amidst the materials through which it is commonly made, the friction is so violent, that not only the rust, but the metal too is lost in the progress.'

'Give me leave to correct the expression of your metaphor,' said Mr. Silton: 'that is not always rust which is acquired by the inactivity of the body on which it preys; such, perhaps, is the case with me, though indeed I was never cleared from my youth; but (taking it in its first stage) it is rather an encrustation, which nature has given for purposes of the greatest wisdom.'

'You are right,' I returned; 'and sometimes, like certain precious fossils, there may be hid under it gems of the purest brilliancy.'

'Nay, farther,' continued Mr. Silton, 'there are two distinct sorts of what we call bashfulness; this, the aukwardness of a booby, which a few steps into the world will convert into the pertness of a coxcomb; that, a consciousness, which the most delicate feelings produce, and the most extensive knowledge cannot always remove.'

From the incidents I have already related, I imagine it will be concluded, that Harley was of the latter species of bashful animals; at least, if Mr. Silton's principle is just, it may be argued on this side: for the gradation of the first mentioned sort, it is certain, he never attained. Some part of his external appearance was modelled from the company of those gentlemen, whom the antiquity of a family, now possessed of bare 250 l. a year,* entitled its representative to approach; these indeed were not many; great part of the property in his neighbourhood being in the hands of merchants, who had got rich by their lawful calling abroad, and the sons of stewards, who had got rich by their lawful calling at home: persons so perfectly versed in the ceremonial of thousands, tens of thousands, and hundreds of thousands (whose degrees of precedency are plainly demonstrable from the first page of the Compleat Accomptant, or Young Man's best Pocket Companion) that a bow at church from them to such a man as Harley,—would have made the person look back into his sermon for some precept of Christian humility.

CHAPTER XII

OF WORLDLY INTERESTS

THERE are certain interests which the world supposes every man to have, and which therefore are properly enough termed worldly; but the world is apt to make an erroneous estimate: ignorant of the dispositions which constitute our happiness or misery, they bring to an undistinguished scale the means of the one, as connected with power, wealth, or grandeur, and of the other with their contraries. Philosophers and poets have often protested against this decision; but their arguments have been despised as declamatory, or ridiculed as romantic.

There are never wanting to a young man some grave and prudent friends to set him right in this particular, if he need it: to watch his ideas as they arise, and point them to those objects which a wise man should never forget.

Harley did not want for some monitors of this sort. He was frequently told of men, whose fortunes enabled them to command all the luxuries of life, whose fortunes were of their own acquirement: his envy was invited by a description of their happiness, and his emulation by a recital of the means which had procured it.

Harley was apt to hear those lectures with indifference; nay

sometimes they got the better of his temper; and as the instances
were not always amiable, provoked, on his part, some reflections,
which I am persuaded his good-nature would else have avoided.

Indeed I have observed one ingredient, somewhat necessary in
a man's composition towards happiness, which people of feeling
would do well to acquire; a certain respect for the follies of mankind: for there are so many fools whom the opinion of the world
entitles to regard, whom accident has placed in heights of which
they are unworthy, that he who cannot restrain his contempt or
indignation at the sight, will be too often quarrelling with the
disposal of things, to relish that share which is allotted to himself.
I do not mean, however, to insinuate this to have been the case
with Harley; on the contrary, if we might rely on his own testi-
mony, the conceptions he had of pomp and grandeur, served to
endear the state which Providence had assigned him.

He lost his father, the last surviving of his parents, as I have
already related, when he was a boy. The good man, from a fear of
offending, as well as a regard to his son, had named him a variety
of guardians; one consequence of which was, that they seldom
met at all to consider the affairs of their ward; and when they did
meet, their opinions were so opposite, that the only possible
method of conciliation, was the mediatory power of a dinner and
a bottle, which commonly interrupted, not ended, the dispute;
and after that interruption ceased, left the consulting parties in a
condition not very proper for adjusting it. His education therefore had been but indifferently attended to; and after being taken
from a country school, at which he had been boarded, the young
gentleman was suffered to be his own master in the subsequent
branches of literature, with some assistance from the parson of
the parish in languages and philosophy, and from the exciseman
in arithmetic and book-keeping. One of his guardians indeed,
who, in his youth, had been an inhabitant of the Temple, set him
to read Coke upon Lyttelton;* a book which is very properly put
into the hands of beginners in that science, as its simplicity is
accommodated to their understandings, and its size to their
inclination. He profited but little by the perusal; but it was not
without its use in the family: for his maiden aunt applied it

commonly to the laudable purpose of pressing her rebellious linens to the folds she had allotted them.

There were particularly two ways of increasing his fortune, which might have occurred to people of less foresight than the counsellors we have mentioned. One of these was the prospect of his succeeding to an old lady, a distant relation, who was known to be possessed of a very large sum in the stocks: but in this their hopes were disappointed; for the young man was so untoward in his disposition, that, notwithstanding the instructions he daily received, his visits rather tended to alienate than gain the good-will of his kinswoman. He sometimes looked grave when the old lady told the jokes of her youth; he often refused to eat when she pressed him, and was seldom or never provided with sugar-candy or liquorice when she was seized with a fit of coughing: nay, he had once the rudeness to fall asleep, while she was describing the composition and virtues of her favourite cholic-water.* In short, he accommodated himself so ill to her humour, that she died, and did not leave him a farthing.

The other method pointed out to him was, an endeavour to get a lease of some crown-lands,* which lay contiguous to his little paternal estate. This, it was imagined, might be easily procured, as the crown did not draw so much rent as Harley could afford to give, with very considerable profit to himself; and the then lessee had rendered himself so obnoxious to the ministry, by the disposal of his vote at an election, that he could not expect a renewal. This, however, needed some interest with the great, which Harley or his father never possessed.

His neighbour, Mr. Walton, having heard of this affair, generously offered his assistance to accomplish it. He told him, that though he had long been a stranger to courtiers, yet he believed, there were some of them who might pay regard to his recommendation; and that, if he thought it worth the while to take a London-journey upon the business, he would furnish him with a letter of introduction to a baronet of his acquaintance, who had a great deal to say with the first lord of the treasury.

When his friends heard of this offer, they pressed him with the utmost earnestness to accept of it. They did not fail to enumerate

the many advantages which a certain degree of spirit and assurance gives a man who would make a figure in the world: they
repeated their instances of good fortune in others, ascribed them
all to a happy forwardness of disposition; and made so copious a
recital of the disadvantages which attend the opposite weakness,
that a stranger, who had heard them, would have been led to
imagine, that in the British code there was some disqualifying sta-
tute against any citizen who should be convicted of——modesty.

Harley, though he had no great relish for the attempt, yet could
not resist the torrent of motives that assaulted him; and as he
needed but little preparation for his journey, a day, not very
distant, was fixed for his departure.

CHAPTER XIII

THE MAN OF FEELING IN LOVE

THE day before that on which he set out, he went to take leave of
Mr. Walton.—We would conceal nothing;—there was another
person of the family to whom also the visit was intended, on
whose account, perhaps, there were some tenderer feelings in the
bosom of Harley, than his gratitude for the friendly notice of that
gentleman (though he was seldom deficient in that virtue) could
inspire. Mr. Walton had a daughter; and such a daughter! we will
attempt some description of her by and by.

Harley's notions of the καλον,* or beautiful, were not always to
be defined, nor indeed such as the world would always assent to,
though we could define them. A blush, a phrase of affability to an
inferior, a tear at a moving tale, were to him, like the Cestus of
Cytherea,* unequalled in conferring beauty. For all these Miss
Walton was remarkable; but as these, like the above-mentioned
Cestus, are perhaps still more powerful, when the wearer is
possessed of some degree of beauty, commonly so called; it happened, that, from this cause, they had more than usual power in
the person of that young lady.

She was now arrived at that period of life which takes, or is

supposed to take, from the flippancy of girlhood those sprightli-
nesses with which some good-natured old maids oblige the world
at three-score. She had been ushered into life (as that word is
used in the dialect of St. Jameses*) at seventeen, her father being
then in parliament, and living in London: at seventeen, therefore,
she had been a universal toast; her health, now she was four and
twenty was only drank by those who knew her face at least. Her
complexion was mellowed into a paleness, which certainly took
from her beauty; but agreed, at least Harley used to say so, with
the pensive softness of her mind. Her eyes were of that gentle
hazel-colour which is rather mild than piercing; and, except
when they were lighted up by good-humour, which was frequently the case, were supposed by the fine gentlemen to want
fire. Her air and manner were elegant in the highest degree, and
were as sure of commanding respect, as their mistress was far
from demanding it. Her voice was inexpressibly soft; it was,
according to that incomparable simile of Otway's.*

——'like the shepherd's pipe upon the mountains,
'When all his little flock's at feed before him.'

The effect it had upon Harley, himself used to paint ridiculously
enough; and ascribed to it powers, which few believed, and
nobody cared for.

Her conversation was always cheerful, but rarely witty; and
without the smallest affectation of learning, had as much sentiment in it as would have puzzled a Turk, upon his principles of
female materialism,* to account for. Her beneficence was
unbounded; indeed the natural tenderness of her heart might
have been argued, by the frigidity of a casuist, as detracting from
her virtue in this respect, for her humanity was a feeling, not a
principle: but minds like Harley's are not very apt to make this
distinction, and generally give our virtue credit for all that
benevolence which is instinctive in our nature.

As her father had some years retired to the country, Harley had
frequent opportunities of seeing her. He looked on her for some
time merely with that respect and admiration which her appearance seemed to demand, and the opinion of others conferred

upon her: from this cause perhaps, and from that extreme sensibility of which we have taken frequent notice, Harley was remarkably silent in her presence. He heard her sentiments with peculiar attention, sometimes with looks very expressive of approbation; but seldom declared his opinion on the subject, much less made compliments to the lady on the justness of her remarks.

From this very reason it was, that Miss Walton frequently took more particular notice of him than of other visitors, who, by the laws of precedency, were better entitled to it: it was a mode of politeness she had peculiarly studied, to bring to the line of that equality, which is ever necessary for the ease of our guests, those whose sensibility had placed them below it.

Harley saw this; for though he was a child in the drama of the world, yet was it not altogether owing to a want of knowledge in his part; on the contrary, the most delicate consciousness of propriety often kindled that blush which marred the performance of it: this raised his esteem something above what the most sanguine descriptions of her goodness had been able to do; for certain it is, that notwithstanding the laboured definitions which very wise men have given us of the inherent beauty of virtue, we are always inclined to think her handsomest when she condescends to smile upon ourselves.

It would be trite to observe the easy gradation from esteem to love; in the bosom of Harley there scarce needed a transition; for there were certain seasons when his ideas were flushed to a degree much above their common complexion. In times not credulous of inspiration, we should account for this from some natural cause; but we do not mean to account for it at all; it were sufficient to describe its effects; but they were sometimes so ludicrous, as might derogate from the dignity of the sensations which produced them to describe. They were treated indeed as such by most of Harley's sober friends, who often laughed very heartily at the aukward blunders of the real Harley, when the different faculties, which should have prevented them, were entirely occupied by the ideal. In some of these paroxisms of fancy, Miss Walton did not fail to be introduced; and the picture which had been drawn amidst the surrounding objects of unnoticed levity, was now singled out to be viewed through the medium of romantic imagination: it was improved of course, and esteem was a word inexpressive of the feelings which it excited.

CHAPTER XIV

HE SETS OUT ON HIS JOURNEY—THE BEGGAR AND HIS DOG

HE had taken leave of his aunt on the eve of his intended departure; but the good lady's affection for her nephew interrupted her sleep, and early as it was next morning when Harley came down stairs to set out, he found her in the parlour with a tear on her cheek, and her caudle-cup* in her hand. She knew enough of physic to prescribe against going abroad of a morning with an empty stomach. She gave her blessing with the draught; her instructions she had delivered the night before. They consisted mostly of negatives; for London, in her idea, was so replete with temptations, that it needed the whole armour of her friendly cautions to repel their attacks.

Peter stood at the door. We have mentioned this faithful fellow formerly: Harley's father had taken him up an orphan, and saved him from being cast on the parish; and he had ever since remained in the service of him and of his son. Harley shook him by the hand as he passed, smiling, as if he had said, 'I will not weep.' He sprung hastily into the chaise that waited for him: Peter folded up the step. 'My dear master,' said he, (shaking the solitary lock that hung on either side of his head) 'I have been told as how London is a sad place.'—He was choked with the thought, and his benediction could not be heard:—but it shall be heard, honest Peter!—where these tears will add to its energy.

In a few hours Harley reached the inn where he proposed breakfasting; but the fulness of his heart would not suffer him to eat a morsel. He walked out on the road, and gaining a little height, stood gazing on that quarter he had left. He looked for his wonted prospect, his fields, his woods, and his hills: they were lost in the distant clouds! He pencilled them on the clouds, and bade them farewel with a sigh!

He sat down on a large stone to take out a little pebble from his shoe, when he saw, at some distance, a beggar approaching him. He had on a loose sort of coat, mended with different-coloured rags, amongst which the blue and the russet were predominant. He had a short knotty stick in his hand, and on the top of it was stuck a ram's horn; his knees (though he was no pilgrim) had worn the stuff of his breeches; he wore no shoes, and his stockings had entirely lost that part of them which should have covered his feet and ancles: in his face, however, was the plump appearance of good-humour; he walked a good round pace, and a crook-legged dog trotted at his heels.

'Our delicacies,' said Harley to himself, 'are fantastic; they are not in nature! that beggar walks over the sharpest of these stones barefooted, while I have lost the most delightful dream in the world, from the smallest of them happening to get into my shoe.'—The beggar had by this time come up, and pulling off a piece of hat, asked charity of Harley; the dog began to beg too:— it was impossible to resist both; and in truth, the want of shoes and stockings had made both unnecessary, for Harley had destined sixpence for him before. The beggar, on receiving it, poured forth blessings without number; and, with a sort of smile on his countenance, said to Harley, 'that, if he wanted to have his fortune told'—Harley turned his eye briskly on the beggar: it was an unpromising look for the subject of a prediction, and silenced the prophet immediately. 'I would much rather learn,' said Harley, 'what it is in your power to tell me: your trade must be an entertaining one: sit down on this stone, and let me know something of your profession; I have often thought of turning fortune-teller for a week or two myself.'

'Master,' replied the beggar, 'I like your frankness much; God knows I had the humour of plain-dealing in me from a child; but there is no doing with it in this world; we must live as we can, and lying is, as you call it, my profession: but I was in some sort forced to the trade, for I dealt once in telling truth.

'I was a labourer, Sir, and gained as much as to make me live: I never laid by indeed; for I was reckoned a piece of a wag, and your wags, I take it, are seldom rich, Mr. Harley.' 'So,' said Harley, 'you seem to know me.' 'Ay, there are few folks in the country that I don't know something of: How should I tell fortunes else?' 'True; but to go on with your story: you were a labourer, you say, and a wag; your industry, I suppose, you left with your old trade; but your humour you preserve to be of use to you in your new.'

'What signifies sadness, Sir? a man grows lean on't: but I was brought to my idleness by degrees; first I could not work, and it went against my stomach to work ever after. I was seized with a jail-fever at the time of the assizes being in the county where I lived; for I was always curious to get acquainted with the felons, because they are commonly fellows of much mirth and little thought, qualities I had ever an esteem for. In the height of this fever, Mr. Harley, the house where I lay took fire, and burnt to the ground: I was carried out in that condition, and lay all the rest of my ilness in a barn. I got the better of my disease however, but I was so weak that I spit blood whenever I attempted to work. I had no relation living that I knew of, and I never kept a friend above a week, when I was able to joke; I seldom remained above six months in a parish, so that I might have died before I had found a settlement in any: thus I was forced to beg my bread, and a sorry trade I found it, Mr. Harley. I told all my misfortunes truly, but they were seldom believed; and the few who gave me a half-penny as they passed, did it with a shake of the head, and an injunction, not to trouble them with a long story. In short, I found that people don't care to give alms without some security for their money; a wooden leg or a withered arm is a sort of draught upon heaven for those who chuse to have their money placed to account there; so I changed my plan, and, instead of telling my own misfortunes, began to prophesy happiness to others. This I found by much the better way: folks will always listen when the tale is their own; and of many who say they do not believe in fortune-telling, I have known few on whom it had not a very sensible effect. I pick up the names of their acquaintance; amours and little squabbles are easily gleaned among servants and neigh-bours; and indeed people themselves are the best intelligencers in the world for our purpose: they dare not puzzle us for their own sakes, for every one is anxious to hear what they wish to believe; and they who repeat it to laugh at it when they have done, are generally more serious than their hearers are apt to imagine. With a tolerable good memory, and some share of cunning, with the help of walking a-nights over heaths and church-yards, with this, and shewing the tricks of that there dog, whom I stole from the serjeant of a marching regiment (and by the way he can steal too upon occasion) I make shift to pick up a livelihood. My trade, indeed, is none of the honestest; yet people are not much cheated neither, who give a few halfpence for a prospect of happiness, which I have heard some persons say is all a man can arrive at in this world.—But I must bid you good-day, Sir; for I have three miles to walk before noon, to inform some boarding-school young ladies, whether their husbands are to be peers of the realm, or captains in the army: a question which I promised to answer them by that time.'

Harley had drawn a shilling from his pocket; but virtue bade him consider on whom he was going to bestow it.—Virtue held back his arm:—but a milder form, a younger sister of virtue's, not so severe as virtue, nor so serious as pity, smiled upon him: His fingers lost their compression;—nor did virtue offer to catch the money as it fell. It had no sooner reached the ground than the watchful cur (a trick he had been taught) snapped it up; and, contrary to the most approved method of stewardship, delivered it immediately into the hands of his master.

Virtue- reason, not Charity

CHAPTER XIX

HE MAKES A SECOND EXPEDITION TO THE BARONET'S. THE LAUDABLE AMBITION OF A YOUNG MAN TO BE THOUGHT SOMETHING BY THE WORLD

WE have related, in a former chapter, the little success of his first visit to the great man, for whom he had the introductory letter from Mr. Walton. To people of equal sensibility, the influence of those trifles we mentioned on his deportment will not appear surprising; but to his friends in the country, they could not be stated, nor would they have allowed them any place in the account. In some of their letters, therefore, which he received soon after, they expressed their surprise at his not having been more urgent in his application, and again recommended the blushless assiduity of successful merit.

He resolved to make another attempt at the baronet's; fortified with higher notions of his own dignity, and with less apprehension of repulse.* In his way to Grosvenor-square he began to ruminate on the folly of mankind, who affixed those ideas of superiority to riches, which reduced the minds of men, by nature equal with the more fortunate, to that sort of servility which he felt in his own. By the time he had reached the Square, and was walking along the pavement which led to the baronet's, he had brought his reasoning on the subject to such a point, that the conclusion, by every rule of logic, should have led him to a thorough indifference in his approaches to a fellow-mortal, whether that fellow-mortal was possessed of six, or six thousand pounds a year. It is probable, however, that the premises had been improperly formed; for it is certain, that when he approached the great man's door, he felt his heart agitated by an unusual pulsation.

He had almost reached it, when he observed a young gentleman coming out, dressed in a white frock, and a red laced waistcoat, with a small switch in his hand, which he seemed to manage with a particular good grace. As he passed him on the steps, the stranger very politely made him a bow, which Harley returned, though he could not remember ever having seen him before. He asked Harley, in the same civil manner, if he was going to wait on his friend the Baronet? 'For I was just calling,' said he, 'and am sorry to find that he is gone for some days into the country.' Harley thanked him for his information; and was turning from the door, when the other observed, that it would be proper to leave his name and very obligingly knocked for that purpose. 'Here is a gentleman, Tom, who meant to have waited on your master.' 'Your name, if you please, Sir?' 'Harley.'—'You'll remember, Tom, Harley.'—The door was shut. 'Since we are here,' said he, 'we shall not lose our walk, if we add a little to it by a turn or two in Hyde-park.' He accompanied this proposal with a second bow, and Harley accepted of it by another in return.

The conversation, as they walked, was brilliant on the side of his companion. The playhouse, the opera, with every occurrence in high-life, he seemed perfectly master of; and talked of some reigning beauties of quality, in a manner the most feeling in the world. Harley admired the happiness of his vivacity; and, opposite as it was to the reserve of his own nature, began to be much pleased with its effects.

Though I am not of opinion with some wise men, that the existence of objects depends on idea;* yet, I am convinced, that their appearance is not a little influenced by it. The optics of some minds are in so unlucky a perspective, as to throw a certain shade on every picture that is presented to them; while those of others (of which number was Harley) like the mirrors of the ladies, have a wonderful effect in bettering their complexions. Through such a medium perhaps he was looking on his present companion.

When they had finished their walk, and were returning by the corner of the Park, they observed a board hung out of a window, signifying, 'An excellent ORDINARY* on Saturdays and Sundays.' It happened to be Saturday, and the table was covered for the purpose. 'What if we should go in and dine here, if you happen not to be engaged, Sir?' said the young gentleman. 'It is not impossible but we shall meet with some original or other; it is a sort of humour I like hugely.' Harley made no objection; and the stranger showed him the way into the parlour.

He was placed, by the courtesy of his introductor, in an arm-chair that stood at one side of the fire. Over-against him was seated a man of a grave considering aspect, with that look of sober prudence which indicates what is commonly called a warm man. He wore a pretty large wig, which had once been white, but was now of a brownish yellow; his coat was one of those modest-coloured drabs which mock the injuries of dust and dirt; two jack-boots concealed, in part, the well-mended knees of an old pair of buckskin breeches, while the spotted handkerchief round his neck, preserved at once its owner from catching cold, and his neckcloth from being dirtied. Next him sat another man, with a tankard in his hand, and a quid of tobacco in his cheek, whose eye was rather more vivacious, and whose dress was something smarter.

The first-mentioned gentleman took notice, that the room had been so lately washed, as not to have had time to dry; and remarked, that wet lodging was unwholesome for man or beast. He looked round at the same time for a poker to stir the fire with, which, he at last observed to the company, the people of the house had removed, in order to save their coals. This difficulty, however, he overcame, by the help of Harley's stick, saying, 'that as they should, no doubt, pay for their fire in some shape or other, he saw no reason why they should not have the use of it while they sat.'

The door was now opened for the admission of dinner. 'I don't know how it is with you, gentlemen,' said Harley's new acquaintance; 'but I am afraid I shall not be able to get down a morsel at this horrid mechanical hour of dining.' He sat down, however, and did not show any want of appetite by his eating. He took upon him the carving of the meat, and criticised on the goodness of the pudding.

When the table-cloth was removed, he proposed calling for some punch, which was readily agreed to; he seemed at first inclined to make it himself, but afterwards changed his mind, and left that province to the waiter, telling him to have it pure West-Indian,* or he could not taste a drop of it.

When the punch was brought, he undertook to fill the glasses and call the toasts.—'The king.'—The toast naturally produced politics. It is the privilege of Englishmen to drink the king's health, and to talk of his conduct. The man who sat opposite to Harley (and who by this time, partly from himself, and partly from his acquaintance on his left hand, was discovered to be a grazier) observed, 'That it was a shame for so many pensioners to be allowed to take the bread out of the mouth of the poor.' 'Ay, and provisions,' said his friend, 'were never so dear in the memory of man; I wish the king, and his counsellors, would look to that.' 'As for the matter of provisions, neighbour Wrightson,' he replied, 'I am sure the prices of cattle—' A dispute would have probably ensued, but it was prevented by the spruce toast-master, who gave a Sentiment: and turning to the two politicians, 'Pray, gentlemen,' said he, 'let us have done with these musty politics: I would always leave them to the beer-suckers in Butcher-row.* Come, let us have something of the fine arts. That was a damn'd hard match betwixt the Nailor and Tim Bucket.* The knowing ones were cursedly taken in there! I lost a cool hundred myself, faith.'

At mention of the cool hundred, the grazier threw his eyes aslant, with a mingled look of doubt and surprise; while the man at his elbow looked arch, and gave a short emphatical sort of cough.

Both seemed to be silenced, however, by this intelligence; and, while the remainder of the punch lasted, the conversation was wholly engrossed by the gentleman with the fine waistcoat, who told a great many 'immense comical stories,' and 'confounded smart things,' as he termed them, acted and spoken by lords, ladies, and young bucks of quality, of his acquaintance. At last, the grazier, pulling out a watch, of a very unusual size, and telling the hour, said, that he had an appointment. 'Is it so late?' said the young gentleman; 'then I am afraid I have missed an appointment already; but the truth is, I am cursedly given to missing of appointments.'

When the grazier and he were gone, Harley turned to the remaining personage, and asked him, If he knew that young gentleman? 'A gentleman!' said he; 'ay, he is one of your gentle-men at the top of an affidavit. I knew him, some years ago, in the quality of a footman; and, I believe, he had sometimes the honour to be a pimp. At last, some of the great folks, to whom he had been serviceable in both capacities, had him made a gauger* in which station he remains, and has the assurance to pretend an acquaintance with men of quality. The impudent dog! with a few shillings in his pocket, he will talk you three times as much as my friend Mundy there, who is worth nine thousand, if he's worth a farthing. But I know the rascal, and despise him, as he deserves.'

Harley began to despise him too, and to conceive some indignation at having sat with patience to hear such a fellow speak nonsense. But he corrected himself, by reflecting, that he was perhaps as well entertained, and instructed too, by this same modest gauger, as he should have been by such a man as he had thought proper to personate. And surely the fault may more properly be imputed to that rank where the futility is real, than where it is feigned; to that rank, whose opportunities for nobler accomplishments have only served to rear a fabric of folly, which the untutored hand of affectation, even among the meanest of mankind, can imitate with success.

CHAPTER XX

HE VISITS BEDLAM*—THE DISTRESSES OF A DAUGHTER

OF those things called Sights, in London, which every stranger is supposed desirous to see, Bedlam is one. To that place, therefore, an acquaintance of Harley's, after having accompanied him to several other shows, proposed a visit. Harley objected to it, 'because,' said he, 'I think it an inhuman practice to expose the greatest misery with which our nature is afflicted, to every idle visitant who can afford a trifling perquisite to the keeper; especially as it is a distress which the humane must see with the painful reflection, that it is not in their power to alleviate it.' He was overpowered, however, by the solicitations of his friend, and the other persons of the party (amongst whom were several ladies); and they went in a body to Moorfields.

Their conductor led them first to the dismal mansions of those who are in the most horrid state of incurable madness. The clanking of chains, the wildness of their cries, and the imprecations which some of them uttered, formed a scene inexpressibly shocking. Harley and his companions, especially the female part of them, begged their guide to return: he seemed surprised at their uneasiness, and was with difficulty prevailed on to leave that part of the house without showing them some others; who, as he expressed it in the phrase of those that keep wild beasts for a shew, were much better worth seeing than any they had passed, being ten times more fierce and unmanageable.

He led them next to that quarter where those reside, who, as they are not dangerous to themselves or others, enjoy a certain degree of freedom, according to the state of their distemper.

Harley had fallen behind his companions, looking at a man, who was making pendulums with bits of thread, and little balls of clay. He had delineated a segment of a circle on the wall with chalk, and marked their different vibrations, by intersecting it with cross lines. A decent-looking man came up, and smiling at the maniac, turned to Harley, and told him, that gentleman had once been a very celebrated mathematician. 'He fell a sacrifice,' said he, 'to the theory of comets; for, having, with infinite labour, formed a table on the conjectures of Sir Isaac Newton,* he was disappointed in the return of one of those luminaries, and was very soon after obliged to be placed here by his friends. If you please to follow me, Sir,' continued the stranger, 'I believe I shall be able to give you a more satisfactory account of the unfortunate people you see here, than the man who attends your companions.' Harley bowed, and accepted his offer.

The next person they came up to had scrawled a variety of figures on a piece of slate. Harley had the curiosity to take a nearer view of them. They consisted of different columns, on the top of which were marked South-sea annuities, India-stock,* and Three per cent. annuities consol. 'This,' said Harley's instructor, 'was a gentleman well known in Change-alley. He was once worth fifty thousand pounds, and had actually agreed for the purchase of an estate in the west, in order to realize his money; but he quarrelled with the proprietor about the repairs of the garden-wall, and so returned to town to follow his old trade of stock-jobbing a little longer; when an unlucky fluctuation of stock, in which he was engaged to an immense extent, reduced him at once to poverty and to madness. Poor wretch! he told me t'other day, that against the next payment of differences, he should he some hundreds above a plum.'*

'It is a spondee, and I will maintain it,' interrupted a voice on his left hand. This assertion was followed by a very rapid recital of some verses from Homer. 'That figure,' said the gentleman, 'whose clothes are so bedaubed with snuff, was a schoolmaster of some reputation: he came hither to be resolved of some doubts he entertained concerning the genuine pronunciation of the Greek vowels. In his highest fits, he makes frequent mention of one Mr. Bentley.*

'But delusive ideas, Sir, are the motives of the greatest part of mankind, and a heated imagination the power by which their actions are incited: the world, in the eye of a philosopher, may be said to be a large madhouse.' 'It is true,' answered Harley, 'the passions of men are temporary madnesses; and sometimes very fatal in their effects,

From Macedonia's madman to the Swede.'*

'It was indeed,' said the stranger, 'a very mad thing in Charles, to think of adding so vast a country as Russia to his dominions; that would have been fatal indeed; the balance of the North would then have been lost; but the Sultan and I would never have allowed it.'—'Sir!' said Harley, with no small surprise on his countenance. 'Why, yes,' answered the other, 'the Sultan and I; do you know me? I am the Chan of Tartary.'*

Harley was a good deal struck by this discovery; he had prudence enough, however, to conceal his amazement, and bowing as low to the monarch as his dignity required, left him immediately, and joined his companions.

He found them in a quarter of the house set apart for the insane of the other sex, several of whom had gathered about the female visitors, and were examining, with rather more accuracy than might have been expected, the particulars of their dress.

Separate from the rest stood one, whose appearance had something of superior dignity. Her face, though pale and wasted, was less squalid than those of the others, and showed a dejection of that decent kind, which moves our pity unmixed with horror: upon her, therefore, the eyes of all were immediately turned. The keeper, who accompanied them, observed it: 'This,' said he, 'is a young lady, who was born to ride in her coach and six. She was beloved, if the story I have heard is true, by a young gentleman, her equal in birth, though by no means her match in fortune: but Love, they say, is blind, and so she fancied him as much as he did her. Her father, it seems, would not hear of their marriage, and threatened to turn her out of doors, if ever she saw him again. Upon this the young gentleman took a voyage to the West Indies, in hopes of bettering his fortune, and obtaining his mistress; but he was scarce landed, when he was seized with one of the fevers which are common in those islands, and died in a few days, lamented by every one that knew him. This news soon reached his mistress, who was at the same time pressed by her father to marry a rich miserly fellow, who was old enough to be her grandfather. The death of her lover had no effect on her inhuman parent; he was only the more earnest for her marriage with the man he had provided for her; and what between her despair at the death of the one, and her aversion to the other, the poor young lady was reduced to the condition you see her in. But God would not prosper such cruelty; her father's affairs soon after went to wreck, and he died almost a beggar.'

Though this story was told in very plain language, it had particularly attracted Harley's notice: he had given it the tribute of some tears. The unfortunate young lady had till now seemed entranced in thought, with her eyes fixed on a little garnet-ring she wore on her finger: she turned them now upon Harley. 'My Billy is no more!' said she, 'do you weep for my Billy? Blessings on your tears! I would weep too, but my brain is dry; and it burns, it burns, it burns!'—She drew nearer to Harley. —'Be comforted, young Lady,' said he, 'your Billy is in heaven.' 'Is he, indeed? and shall we meet again? And shall that frightful man' (pointing to the keeper) 'not be there?—Alas! I am grown naughty of late; I have almost forgotten to think of heaven: yet I pray sometimes; when I can, I pray; and sometimes I sing; when I am saddest, I sing:— You shall hear me, hush!

'Light be the earth on Billy's breast,'*
'And green the sod that wraps his grave!'

There was a plaintive wildness in the air not to be withstood; and, except the keeper's, there was not an unmoistened eye around her.

'Do you weep again?' said she; 'I would not have you weep: you are like my Billy; you are, believe me; just so he looked when he gave me this ring; poor Billy! 'twas the last time ever we met!—

''Twas when the seas were roaring—I love you for resembling my Billy; but I shall never love any man like him.'—She stretched out her hand to Harley; he pressed it between both of his, and bathed it with his tears.—'Nay, that is Billy's ring,' said she, 'you cannot have it, indeed; but here is another, look here, which I plaited to-day of some gold-thread from this bit of stuff; will you keep it for my sake? I am a strange girl;—but my heart is harmless: my poor heart! it will burst some day; feel how it beats.'— She press'd his hand to her bosom, then holding her head in the attitude of listening—'Hark! one, two, three! be quiet, thou little trembler; my Billy's is cold!—but I had forgotten the ring.'—She put it on his finger.—'Farewell! I must leave you now.'—She would have withdrawn her hand; Harley held it to his lips.—'I dare not stay longer; my head throbs sadly: farewell!'——She walked with a hurried step to a little apartment at some distance. Harley stood fixed in astonishment and pity! his friend gave money to the keeper.—Harley looked on his ring.—He put a couple of guineas into the man's hand: 'Be kind to that unfortunate'—He burst into tears, and left them.

CHAPTER XXI

THE MISANTHROPIST

THE friend, who had conducted him to Moorfields, called upon him again the next evening. After some talk on the adventures of the preceding day; 'I carried you yesterday,' said he to Harley, 'to visit the mad; let me introduce you to-night, at supper, to one of the wise: but you must not look for any thing of the Socratic pleasantry about him; on the contrary, I warn you to expect the spirit of a Diogenes.* That you may be a little prepared for his extraordinary manner, I will let you into some particulars of his history.

'He is the elder of two sons of a gentleman of considerable estate in the country. Their father died when they were young: both were remarkable at school for quickness of parts, and extent of genius; this had been bred to no profession, because his father's fortune, which descended to him, was thought sufficient to set him above it; the other was put apprentice to an eminent attorney. In this the expectations of his friends were more consulted than his own inclination; for both his brother and he had feelings of that warm kind, that could ill brook a study so dry as the law, especially in that department of it which was allotted to him. But the difference of their tempers made the characteristical distinction between them. The younger, from the gentleness of his nature, bore with patience a situation entirely discordant to his genius and disposition. At times, indeed, his pride would suggest, of how little importance those talents were, which the partiality of his friends had often extolled: they were now incumbrances in a walk of life where the dull and the ignorant passed him at every turn; his fancy and his feeling, were invincible obstacles to eminence in a situation, where his fancy had no room for exertion, and his feeling experienced perpetual disgust.* But these murmurings he never suffered to be heard; and that he might not offend the prudence of those who had been concerned in the choice of his profession, he continued to labour in it several years, 'till, by the death of a relation, he succeeded to an estate of little better than 100 l. a year, with which, and the small patrimony left him, he retired into the country, and made a love-match with a young lady of a temper similar to his own, with whom the sagacious world pitied him for finding happiness.

'But his elder brother, whom you are to see at supper, if you will do us the favour of your company, was naturally impetuous, decisive, and overbearin. He entered into life with those ardent expectations by which young men are commonly deluded: in his friendships, warm to excess; and equally violent in his dislikes. He was on the brink of marriage with a young lady, when one of those friends, for whose honour he would have pawned his life, made an elopement with that very goddess, and left him besides deeply engaged for sums which that good friend's extravagance had squandered.

'The dreams he had formerly enjoyed were now changed for ideas of a very different nature. He abjured all confidence in any thing of human form; sold his lands, which still produced him a very large reversion, came to town, and immured himself with a woman who had been his nurse, in little better than a garret; and has ever since applied his talents to the vilifying of his species. In one thing I must take the liberty to instruct you: however different your sentiments may be (and different they must be) you will suffer him to go on without contradiction; otherwise he will be silent immediately, and we shall not get a word from him all the night after.' Harley promised to remember this injunction, and accepted the invitation of his friend.

When they arrived at the house, they were informed that the gentleman was come, and had been shown into the parlour. They found him sitting with a daughter of his friend's, about three years old, on his knee, whom he was teaching the alphabet from a horn-book:* at a little distance stood a sister of hers, some years older. 'Get you away, Miss,' said he to this last, 'you are a pert gossip, and I will have nothing to do with you.' 'Nay,' answered she, 'Nancy is your favourite; you are quite in love with Nancy.' 'Take away that girl,' said he to her father, whom he now observed to have entered the room, 'she has woman about her already.' The children were accordingly dismissed.

Betwixt that and supper-time he did not utter a syllable. When supper came, he quarrelled with every dish at table, but eat of them all; only exempting from his censures a sallad, 'which you have not spoiled,' said he, 'because you have not attempted to cook it.'

When the wine was set upon the table, he took from his pocket a particular smoking apparatus, and filled his pipe, without taking any more notice of Harley or his friend, than if no such persons had been in the room.

Harley could not help stealing a look of surprize at him; but his friend, who knew his humour, returned it, by annihilating

his presence in the like manner, and, leaving him to his own
mediations, addressed himself entirely to Harley.

In their discourse some mention happened to be made of an
amiable character, and the words *honour* and *politeness* were
applied to it. Upon this the gentleman, laying down his pipe, and
changing the tone of his countenance, from an ironical grin to
something more intently contemptuous: 'Honour,' said he,
'Honour and Politeness! this is the coin of the world, and passes
current with the fools of it. You have substituted the shadow
Honour, instead of the substance Virtue; and have banished the
reality of Friendship for the fictitious semblance, which you have
termed Politeness: politeness, which consists in a certain ceremo-
nious jargon, more ridiculous to the ear of reason than the voice
of a puppet. You have invented sounds, which you worship,
though they tyrannize over your peace: and are surrounded with
empty forms, which take from the honest emotions of joy, and
add to the poignancy of misfortune.'—'Sir,' said Harley—His
friend winked to him, to remind him of the caution he had
received. He was silenced by the thought—The philosopher
turned his eye upon him: he examined him from top to toe, with a
sort of triumphant contempt. Harley's coat happened to be a new
one; the other's was as shabby as could possibly be supposed to be
on the back of a gentleman: there was much significance in his
look with regard to this coat: it spoke of the sleekness of folly, and
the threadbareness of wisdom.

'Truth,' continued he, 'the most amiable, as well as the most
natural of virtues, you are at pains to eradicate. Your very nurser-
ies are seminaries of falsehood; and what is called Fashion in
manhood completes the system of avowed insincerity. Mankind,
in the gross, is a gaping monster, that loves to be deceived, and
has seldom been disappointed: nor is their vanity less fallacious to
your philosophers, who adopt modes of truth to follow them
through the paths of error, and defend paradoxes merely to be
singular in defending them. These are they whom ye term
Ingenious; 'tis a phrase of commendation I detest; it implies an
attempt to impose on my judgment, by flattering my imagination:
yet these are they whose works are read by the old with delight,

which the young are taught to look upon as the codes of knowledge and philosophy.

'Indeed, the education of your youth is every way prepos-
terous: you waste at school years in improving talents, without
having ever spent an hour in discovering them; one promiscuous
line of instruction is followed, without regard to genius, capacity,
or probable situation in the commonwealth. From this bear-
garden of the pedagogue, a raw unprincipled boy is turned loose
upon the world to travel; without any ideas but those of improving
his dress at Paris, or starting into taste by gazing on some paint-
ings at Rome. Ask him of the manners of the people, and he will
tell you, That the skirt is worn much shorter in France, and that
every body eats macaroni in Italy. When he returns home, he buys
a seat in parliament, and studies the constitution at Arthur's.*

'Nor are your females trained to any more useful purpose: they
are taught, by the very rewards which their nurses propose for
good behaviour, by the first thing like a jest which they hear from
every male visitor of the family, that a young woman is a creature
to be married; and when they are grown somewhat older, are
instructed, that it is the purpose of marriage to have the enjoyment of pin-money, and the expectation of a jointure.'

[1]'These indeed are the effects of luxury, which is perhaps
inseparable from a certain degree of power and grandeur in a
nation. But it is not simply of the progress of luxury that we have
to complain: did its votaries keep in their own sphere of thoughtless dissipation, we might despise them without emotion; but the
frivolous pursuits of pleasure are mingled with the most important concerns of the state; and public enterprize shall sleep till he
who should guide its operation has decided his bets at Newmarket,* or fulfilled his engagement with a favourite-mistress in the
country. We want some man of acknowledged eminence to point

---

[1] Though the Curate could not remember having shown this chapter to any body, I
strongly suspect that these political observations are the work of a later pen than the rest
of this performance. There seems to have been, by some accident, a gap in the manuscript, from the words, 'Expectation of a jointure,' to these, 'In short, man is an animal,'
where the present blank ends; and some other person (for the hand is different, and the
ink whiter) has filled part of it with sentiments of his own. Whoever he was, he seems to
have caught some portion of the spirit of the man he personates.

our counsels with that firmness which the counsels of a great people require. We have hundreds of ministers, who press forward into office, without having ever learned that art which is necessary for every business, the art of thinking; and mistake the petulance, which could give inspiration to smart sarcasms on an obnoxious measure in a popular assembly, for the ability which is to balance the interest of kingdoms, and investigate the latent sources of national superiority. With the administration of such men the people can never be satisfied; for, besides that their confidence is gained only by the view of superior talents, there needs that depth of knowledge, which is not only acquainted with the just extent of power, but can also trace its connection with the expedient, to preserve its possessors from the contempt which attends irresolution, or the resentment which follows temerity.'

*   *   *   *   *

[Here a considerable part is wanting.]

*   * 'In short, man is an animal equally selfish and vain. Vanity, indeed, is but a modification of selfishness. From the latter, there are some who pretend to be free: they are generally such as declaim against the lust of wealth and power, because they have never been able to attain any high degree in either: they boast of generosity and feeling. They tell us (perhaps they tell us in rhime) that the sensations of an honest heart, of a mind universally benevolent, make up the quiet bliss which they enjoy; but they will not, by this, be exempted from the charge of selfishness. Whence the luxurious happiness they describe in their little family-circles? Whence the pleasure which they feel, when they trim their evening fires, and listen to the howl of winter's wind? whence, but from the secret reflection of what houseless wretches feel from it? Or do you administer comfort in affliction—the motive is at hand; I have had it preached to me in nineteen out of twenty of your consolatory discourses—the comparative littleness of our own misfortunes.

'With vanity your best virtues are grossly tainted: your

benevolence, which ye deduce immediately from the natural impulse of the heart, squints to it for its reward. There are some, indeed, who tell us of the satisfaction which flows from a secret consciousness of good actions: this secret satisfaction is truly excellent—when we have some friend to whom we may discover its excellence.'

He now paus'd a moment to relight his pipe, when a clock, that stood at his back, struck eleven; he started up at the sound, took his hat and his cane, and nodding good-night with his head, walked out of the room. The gentleman of the house called a servant to bring the stranger's surtout. 'What sort of a night is it, fellow?' said he. 'It rains, Sir,' answered the servant, 'with an easterly wind.'—'Easterly for ever!'—He made no other reply; but shrugging up his shoulders till they almost touched his ears, wrapped himself tight in his great coat, and disappeared.

'This is a strange creature,' said his friend to Harley. 'I cannot say,' answered he, 'that his remarks are of the pleasant kind: it is curious to observe how the nature of truth may be changed by the garb it wears; softened to the admonition of friendship, or soured into the severity of reproof: yet this severity may be useful to some tempers; it somewhat resembles a file; disagreeable in its operation, but hard metals may be the brighter for it.'

Harley

* * * * *

CHAPTER XXV

HIS SKILL IN PHYSIOGNOMY

THE company at the baronet's removed to the playhouse accordingly, and Harley took his usual route into the Park. He observed, as he entered, a fresh-looking elderly gentleman, in conversation with a beggar, who, leaning on his crutch, was recounting the hardships he had undergone, and explaining the wretchedness of his present condition. This was a very interesting dialogue to Harley; he was rude enough therefore to slacken his pace as he

approached, and at last to make a full stop at the gentleman's
back, who was just then expressing his compassion for the beggar,
and regretting that he had not a farthing of change about him. At
saying this he looked piteously on the fellow: there was something
in his physiognomy which caught Harley's notice: indeed physiognomy was one of Harley's foibles, for which he had been
often rebuked by his aunt in the country; who used to tell him,
that when he was come to her years and experience, he would
know that all's not gold that glisters: and it must be owned, that
his aunt was a very sensible, harsh-looking, maiden-lady of three-
score and upwards. But he was too apt to forget this caution; and
now, it seems, it had not occurred to him: stepping up, therefore,
to the gentleman, who was lamenting the want of silver, 'Your
intentions, Sir,' said he, 'are so good, that I cannot help lending
you my assistance to carry them into execution,' and gave the
beggar a shilling. The other returned a suitable compliment, and
extolled the benevolence of Harley. They kept walking together,
and benevolence grew the topic of discourse.

The stranger was fluent on the subject. 'There is no use of
money,' said he, 'equal to that of beneficence: with the profuse, it
is lost; and even with those who lay it out according to the prudence of the world, the objects acquired by it pall on the sense,
and have scarce become our own till they lose their value with the
power of pleasing; but here the enjoyment grows on reflection,
and our money is most truly ours, when it ceases being in our
possession.'

'Yet I agree in some measure,' answered Harley, 'with those
who think, that charity to our common beggars is often mis-
placed; there are objects less obtrusive, whose title is a better one.'

'We cannot easily distinguish,' said the stranger; 'and even of
the worthless, are there not many whose impudence, or whose
vice, may have been one dreadful consequence of misfortune?'

Harley looked again in his face, and blessed himself for his skill
in physiognomy.

By this time they had reached the end of the walk: the old
gentleman leaned on the rails to take breath, and in the mean time
they were joined by a younger man, whose figure was much above

the appearance of his dress, which was poor and shabby: Harley's former companion addressed him as an acquaintance, and they turned on the walk together.

The elder of the strangers complained of the closeness of the evening, and asked the other, if he would go with him into a house hard by, and take one draught of excellent cyder. 'The man who keeps this house,' said he to Harley, 'was once a servant of mine: I could not think of turning loose upon the world a faithful old fellow, for no other reason but that his age had incapacitated him; so I give him an annuity of ten pounds, with the help of which he has set up this little place here, and his daughter goes and sells milk in the city, while her father manages his tap-room, as he calls it, at home. I can't well ask a gentleman of your appearance to accompany me to so paltry a place.'—'Sir,' replied Harley, interrupting him, 'I would much rather enter it than the most celebrated tavern in town: to give to the necessitous, may sometimes be a weakness in the man; to encourage industry, is a duty in the citizen.' They entered the house accordingly.

On a table, at the corner of the room, lay a pack of cards, loosely thrown together. The old gentleman reproved the man of the house for encouraging so idle an amusement: Harley attempted to defend him from the necessity of accommodating himself to the humour of his guests, and taking up the cards, began to shuffle them backwards and forwards in his hand. 'Nay, I don't think cards so unpardonable an amusement as some do,' replied the other; 'and now and then, about this time of the evening, when my eyes begin to fail me for my book, I divert myself with a game at piquet,* without finding my morals a bit relaxed by it. Do you play piquet, Sir?' (to Harley.) Harley answered in the affirmative; upon which the other proposed playing a pool at a shilling the game, doubling the stakes: adding, that he never played higher with any body.

Harley's good–nature could not refuse the benevolent old man; and the younger stranger, though he at first pleaded prior engagement, yet being earnestly solicited by his friend, at last yielded to solicitation.

When they began to play, the old gentleman, somewhat to the

surprise of Harley, produced ten shillings to serve for markers of his score. 'He had no change for the beggar,' said Harley to himself; 'but I can easily account for it: it is curious to observe the affection that inanimate things will create in us by a long acquaintance: if I may judge from my own feelings, the old man would not part with one of these counters for ten times its intrinsic value; it even got the better of his benevolence! I myself have a pair of old brass sleeve-buttons—' Here he was interrupted by being told, that the old gentleman had beat the younger, and that it was his turn to take up the conqueror. 'Your game has been short;' said Harley. 'I repiqued him,' answered the old man, with joy sparkling in his countenance. Harley wished to be repiqued too, but he was disappointed; for he had the same good fortune against his opponent. Indeed, never did fortune, mutable as she is, delight in mutability so much as at that moment; the victory was so quick, and so constantly alternate, that the stake, in a short time, amounted to no less a sum than 12 l. Harley's proportion of which was within half a guinea of the money he had in his pocket. He had before proposed a division, but the old gentleman opposed it with such a pleasant warmth in his manner, that it was always over-ruled. Now, however, he told them, that he had an appointment with some gentlemen, and it was within a few minutes of his hour. The young stranger had gained one game, and was engaged in the second with the other: they agreed therefore that the stake should be divided, if the old gentleman won that; which was more than probable, as his score was 90 to 35, and he was elder hand; but a momentous repique decided it in favour of his adversary, who seemed to enjoy his victory mingled with regret, for having won too much, while his friend, with great ebullience of passion, many praises of his own good play, and many maledictions on the power of chance, took up the cards, and threw them into the fire.

CHAPTER XXVI

THE MAN OF FEELING IN A BROTHEL

THE company he was engaged to meet were assembled in Fleet-street. He had walked some time along the Strand, amidst a croud of those wretches who wait the uncertain wages of prostitution, with ideas of pity suitable to the scene around him, and the feelings he possessed, and had got as far as Somerset-house, when one of them laid hold of his arm, and, with a voice tremulous and faint, asked him for a pint of wine, in a manner more supplicatory than is usual with those whom the infamy of their profession has deprived of shame: he turned round at the demand, and looked stedfastly on the person who made it.

She was above the common size, and elegantly formed; her face was thin and hollow, and showed the remains of tarnished beauty. Her eyes were black, but had little of their lustre left: her cheeks had some paint laid on without art, and productive of no advantage to her complexion, which exhibited a deadly paleness on the other parts of her face.

Harley stood in the attitude of hesitation; which she interpreting to her advantage, repeated her request, and endeavoured to force a leer of invitation into her countenance. He took her arm, and they walked on to one of those obsequious taverns in the neighbourhood, where the dearness of the wine is a discharge in full for the character of the house. From what impulse he did this, we do not mean to inquire; as it has ever been against our nature to search for motives where bad ones are to be found.—They entered, and a waiter shewed them a room, and placed a bottle of claret on the table.

Harley filled the lady's glass; which she had no sooner tasted, than dropping it on the floor, and eagerly catching his arm, her eye grew fixed, her lip assumed a clayey whiteness, and she fell back lifeless in her chair.

Harley started from his seat, and, catching her in his arms, supported her from falling to the ground, looking wildly at the door, as if he wanted to run for assistance, but durst not leave the miserable creature. It was not till some minutes after, that it occurred to him to ring the bell, which at last however he thought of, and rung with repeated violence even after the waiter appeared. Luckily the waiter had his senses somewhat more about him; and snatching up a bottle of water, which stood on a buffet at the end of the room, he sprinkled it over the hands and face of the dying figure before him. She began to revive; and with the assistance of some harts-horn drops,* which Harley now for the first time drew from his pocket, was able to desire the waiter to bring her a crust of bread; of which she swallowed some mouthfuls with the appearance of the keenest hunger. The waiter withdrew: when turning to Harley, sobbing at the same time, and shedding tears, 'I am sorry, Sir,' said she, 'that I should have given you so much trouble; but you will pity me when I tell you, that till now I have not tasted a morsel these two days past.'—He fixed his eyes on hers—every circumstance but the last was forgotten; and he took her hand with as much respect as if she had been a dutchess. It was ever the privilege of misfortune to be revered by him.—'Two days!'—said he; 'and I have fared sumptuously every day!'—He was reaching to the bell; she understood his meaning, and prevented him. 'I beg, Sir,' said she, 'that you would give yourself no more trouble about a wretch who does not wish to live; but, at present, I could not eat a bit; my stomach even rose at the last mouthful of that crust.' He offered to call a chair, saying, that he hoped a little rest would relieve her. He had one half-guinea left: 'I am sorry,' he said, 'that at present I should be able to make you an offer of no more than this paltry sum.' She burst into tears! 'Your generosity, Sir, is abused; to bestow it on me is to take it from the virtuous: I have no title but misery to plead; misery of my own procuring.' 'No more of that,' answered Harley; 'there is virtue in these tears; let the fruit of them be virtue.'— He rung, and ordered a chair.—'Though I am the vilest of beings,' said she, 'I have not forgotten every virtue; gratitude, I hope, I shall still have left, did I but know who is my benefactor.'—'My name is Harley'—'Could I ever have an opportunity'—'You shall, and a glorious one too! your future conduct—but I do not mean to reproach you—if, I say—it will be the noblest reward—I will do myself the pleasure of seeing you again.'—Here the waiter entered, and told them the chair was at the door: the lady informed Harley of her lodgings, and he promised to wait on her at ten next morning.

He led her to the chair, and returned to clear with the waiter, without ever once reflecting that he had no money in his pocket. He was ashamed to make an excuse; yet an excuse must be made: he was beginning to frame one, when the waiter cut him short, by telling him, that he could not run scores; but that, if he would leave his watch, or any other pledge, it would be as safe as if it lay in his pocket. Harley jumped at the proposal, and pulling out his watch, delivered it into his hands immediately; and having, for once, had the precaution to take a note of the lodging he intended to visit next morning, sallied forth with a flush of triumph on his face, without taking notice of the sneer of the waiter, who, twirling the watch in his hand, made him a profound bow at the door, and whispered to a girl, who stood in the passage, something, in which the word CULLY* was honoured with a particular emphasis.

CHAPTER XXVII

HIS SKILL IN PHYSIOGNOMY IS DOUBTED

AFTER he had been some time with the company he had appointed to meet, and the last bottle was called for, he first recollected that he should be again at a loss how to discharge his share of the reckoning. He applied therefore to one of them, with whom he was most intimate, acknowledging that he had not a farthing of money about him; and, upon being jocularly asked the reason, acquainted them with the two adventures we have just now related. One of the company asked him, If the old man in Hyde-park did not wear a brownish coat, with a narrow gold-edging, and his companion an old green frock, with a buff-coloured waistcoat? Upon Harley's recollecting that they did; 'Then,' said he, 'you may be thankful you have come off so well;

they are two as noted sharpers, in their way, as any in town, and
but t'other night took me in for a much larger sum: I had some
thoughts of applying to a justice, but one does not like to be seen
in those matters.'

Harley answered, 'That he could not but fancy the gentleman
was mistaken, as he never saw a face promise more honesty than
that of the old man he had met with.'—'His face!' said a grave-
looking man, who sat opposite to him, squirting the juice of his
tobacco obliquely into the grate. There was something very
emphatical in the action; for it was followed by a burst of laughter
round the table. 'Gentlemen,' said Harley, 'you are disposed to be
merry; it may be as you imagine, for I confess myself ignorant of
the town: but there is one thing which makes me bear the loss of
my money with temper; the young fellow who won it, must have
been miserably poor; I observed him borrow money for the stake
from his friend; he had distress and hunger in his countenance:
be his character what it may, his necessities at least plead for
him.'—At this there was a louder laugh than before. 'Gentlemen,' said the lawyer, (one of whose conversations with Harley
we have already recorded) 'here's a very pretty fellow for you: to
have heard him talk some nights ago, as I did, you might have
sworn he was a saint; yet now he games with sharpers, and loses
his money; and is bubbled* by a fine story invented by a whore,
and pawns his watch: here are sanctified doings with a witness!'

'Young gentleman,' said his friend on the other side of the
table, 'let me advise you to be a little more cautious for the future;
and as for faces—you may look into them to know, whether a
man's nose be a long or a short one.'

CHAPTER XXVIII

HE KEEPS HIS APPOINTMENT

THE last night's rallery of his companions was recalled to his
remembrance when he awoke, and the colder homilies of
prudence began to suggest some things which were nowise

favourable for a performance of his promise to the unfortunate female he had met with before. He rose uncertain of his purpose; but the torpor of such considerations was seldom prevalent over the warmth of his nature. He walked some turns backwards and forwards in his room; he recalled the languid form of the fainting wretch to his mind; he wept at the recollection of her tears. 'Though I am the vilest of beings, I have not forgotten every virtue; gratitude, I hope, I shall still have left.'—He took a larger stride—'Powers of mercy that surround me!' cried he, 'do ye not smile upon deeds like these? to calculate the chances of deception is too tedious a business for the life of man!'—The clock struck ten!—When he was got down stairs, he found that he had forgot the note of her lodgings; he gnawed his lips at the delay; he was fairly on the pavement, when he recollected having left his purse; he did but just prevent himself from articulating an imprecation. He rushed a second time up into his chamber. 'What a wretch I am,' said he; 'ere this time perhaps—''Twas a perhaps not to be born:—two vibrations of a pendulum would have served him to lock his bureau;—but they could not be spared.

When he reached the house, and inquired for Miss Atkins, (for that was the lady's name) he was shown up three pair of stairs into a small room lighted by one narrow lattice, and patched round with shreds of different-coloured paper. In the darkest corner stood something like a bed, before which a tattered coverlet hung by way of curtain. He had not waited long when she appeared. Her face had the glister of new-washed tears on it. 'I am ashamed, Sir,' said she, 'that you should have taken this fresh piece of trouble about one so little worthy of it; but, to the humane, I know there is a pleasure in goodness for its own sake: if you have patience for the recital of my story, it may palliate, though it cannot excuse, my faults.' Harley bowed, as a sign of assent; and she began as follows:

'I am the daughter of an officer, whom a service of forty years had advanced no higher than the rank of captain. I have had hints from himself, and been informed by others, that it was in some measure owing to those principles of rigid honour, which it was his boast to possess, and which he early inculcated on me, that he had been able to arrive at no better station. My mother died when I was a child; old enough to grieve for her death, but incapable of remembering her precepts. Though my father was doatingly fond of her, yet there were some sentiments in which they materially differed: She had been bred from her infancy in the strictest principles of religion, and took the morality of her conduct from the motives which an adherence to those principles suggested. My father, who had been in the army from his youth, affixed an idea of pusillanimity to that virtue, which was formed by the doctrines, excited by the rewards, or guarded by the terrors of revelation; his darling idol was the honour of a soldier; a term which he held in such reverence, that he used it for his most sacred asseveration When my mother died, I was some time suffered to continue in those sentiments which her instructions had produced; but soon after, though, from respect to her memory, my father did not absolutely ridicule them, yet he shewed, in his discourse to others, so little regard to them, and, at times, suggested to me motives of action so different, that I was soon weaned from opinions, which I began to consider as the dreams of superstition, or the artful inventions of designing hypocrisy. My mother's books were left behind at the different quarters we removed to, and my reading was principally confined to plays, novels, and those poetical descriptions of the beauty of virtue and honour, which the circulating libraries* easily afforded.

'As I was generally reckoned handsome, and the quickness of my parts extolled by all our visitors, my father had a pride in showing me to the world. I was young, giddy, open to adulation and vain of those talents which acquired it.

'After the last war, my father was reduced to half-pay; with which we retired to a village in the country, which the acquaintance of some genteel families who resided in it, and the cheapness of living, particularly recommended. My father rented a small house, with a piece of ground sufficient to keep a horse for him, and a cow for the benefit of his family. An old man-servant managed his ground; while a maid, who had formerly been my mother's, and had since been mine, undertook the care of our little dairy: they were assisted in each of their provinces by my father and me; and we passed our time in a state of tranquillity, which he had always talked of with delight, and my train of reading had taught me to admire.

'Though I had never seen the polite circles of the metropolis, the company my father had introduced me into had given me a degree of good-breeding, which soon discovered a superiority over the young ladies of our village. I was quoted as an example of politeness, and my company courted by most of the considerable families in the neighbourhood.

'Amongst the houses where I was frequently invited, was Sir George Winbrooke's. He had two daughters nearly of my age, with whom, though they had been bred up in those maxims of vulgar doctrine, which my superior understanding could not but despise, yet as their good-nature led them to an imitation of my manners in every thing else, I cultivated a particular friendship.

'Some months after our first acquaintance, Sir George's eldest son came home from his travels. His figure, his address, and conversation, were not unlike those warm ideas of an accomplished man which my favourite novels had taught me to form; and his sentiments, on the article of religion, were as liberal as my own: when any of these happened to be the topic of our discourse, I, who before had been silent, from a fear of being single in opposition, now kindled at the fire he raised, and defended our mutual opinions with all the eloquence I was mistress of. He would be respectfully attentive all the while; and when I had ended, would raise his eyes from the ground, look at me with a gaze of admiration, and express his applause in the highest strain of encomium. This was an incense the more pleasing, as I seldom or never had met with it before; for the young gentlemen who visited Sir George were for the most part of that athletic order, the pleasure of whose lives is derived from fox-hunting: these are seldom solicitous to please the women at all; or if they were, would never think of applying their flattery to the mind.

'Mr. Winbrooke observed the weakness of my soul, and took every occasion of improving the esteem he had gained. He asked my opinion of every author, of every sentiment, with that submissive diffidence, which shewed an unlimited confidence in my understanding. I saw myself revered, as a superior being, by one whose judgment my vanity told me was not likely to err; preferred by him to all the other visitors of my sex, whose fortunes and rank should have entitled them to a much higher degree of notice: I saw their little jealousies at the distinguished attention he paid me; it was gratitude, it was pride, it was love! Love which had made too fatal a progress in my heart, before any declaration on his part should have warranted a return: but I interpreted every look of attention, every expression of compliment, to the passion I imagined him inspired with, and imputed to his sensibility that silence which was the effect of art and design. At length, however, he took an opportunity of declaring his love: he now expressed himself in such ardent terms, that prudence might have suspected their sincerity; but prudence is rarely found in the situation I had been unguardedly led into; besides, that the course of reading to which I had been accustomed, did not lead me to conclude, that his expressions could be too warm to be sincere: nor was I even alarmed at the manner in which he talked of marriage, a subjection, he often hinted, to which genuine love should scorn to be confined. The woman, he would often say, who had merit like mine to fix his affection, could easily command it for ever. That honour too which I revered, was often called in to enforce his sentiments. I did not, however, absolutely assent to them; but I found my regard for their opposites diminish by degrees. If it is dangerous to be convinced, it is dangerous to listen; for our reason is so much of a machine, that it will not always be able to resist, when the ear is perpetually assailed.

'In short, Mr. Harley, (for I tire you with a relation, the catastrophe of which you will already have imagined) I fell a prey to his artifices. He had not been able so thoroughly to convert me, that my conscience was silent on the subject; but he was so assiduous to give repeated proofs of unabated affection, that I hushed its suggestions as they rose. The world, however, I knew, was not to be silenced; and therefore I took occasion to express my uneasiness to my seducer, and intreat him, as he valued the peace of one to whom he professed such attachment, to remove it by a marriage. He made excuse from his dependence on the will of his father, but quieted my fears by the promise of endeavouring to win his assent.

'My father had been some days absent on a visit to a dying relation, from whom he had considerable expectations. I was left at home, with no other company than my books: my books I found were not now such companions as they used to be: I was restless, melancholy, unsatisfied with myself. But judge my situation when I received a billet from Mr. Winbrooke, informing me, that he had sounded Sir George on the subject we had talked of, and found him so averse to any match so unequal to his own rank and fortune, that he was obliged, with whatever reluctance, to bid adieu to a place, the remembrance of which should ever be dear to him.

'I read this letter a hundred times over. Alone, helpless, conscious of guilt, and abandoned by every better thought, my mind was one motley scene of terror, confusion, and remorse. A thousand expedients suggested themselves, and a thousand fears told me they would be vain: at last, in an agony of despair, I packed up a few clothes, took what money and trinkets were in the house, and set out for London, whither I understood he was gone; pretending to my maid, that I had received letters from my father requiring my immediate attendance. I had no other companion than a boy, a servant to the man from whom I hired my horses. I arrived in London within an hour of Mr. Winbrooke, and accidentally alighted at the very inn where he was.

'He started and turned pale when he saw me; but recovered himself in time enough to make many new protestations of regard, and beg me to make myself easy under a disappointment which was equally afflicting to him. He procured me lodgings, where I slept, or rather endeavoured to sleep, for that night. Next morning I saw him again; he then mildly observed on the imprudence of my precipitate flight from the country, and proposed my removing to lodgings at another end of the town, to elude the search of my father, till he should fall upon some method of excusing my conduct to him, and reconciling him to my return. We took a hackney-coach, and drove to the house he mentioned.

'It was situated in a dirty lane, furnished with a taudry affectation of finery, with some old family-pictures hanging on walls
which their own cobwebs would better have suited. I was struck
with a secret dread at entering; nor was it lessened by the appearance of the landlady, who had that look of selfish shrewdness,
which, of all others, is the most hateful to those whose feelings
are untinctured with the world. A girl, who she told us was her
niece, sat by her, playing on a guitar, while herself was at work,
with the assistance of spectacles, and had a prayer-book, with the
leaves folded down in several places, lying on the table before her.
Perhaps, Sir, I tire you with my minuteness; but the place, and
every circumstance about it, is so impressed on my mind, that I
shall never forget it.

'I dined that day with Mr. Winbrooke alone. He lost by degrees
that restraint which I perceived too well to hang about him
before, and, with his former gaiety and good-humour, repeated
the flattering things, which, though they had once been fatal, I
durst not now distrust. At last, taking my hand and kissing it, "It
is thus," said he, "that love will last, while freedom is preserved;
thus let us ever be blest, without the galling thought that we are
tied to a condition where we may cease to be so." I answered,
"That the world thought otherwise; that it had certain ideas of
good fame, which it was impossible not to wish to maintain."
"The world," said he, "is a tyrant; they are slaves who obey it: let
us be happy without the pale of the world. To-morrow I shall
leave this quarter of it, for one, where the talkers of the world
shall be foiled, and lose us. Could not my Emily accompany me?
my friend, my companion, the mistress of my soul! Nay, do not
look so, Emily! your father may grieve for a while, but your father
shall be taken care of; this bank-bill I intend as the comfort for his
daughter."

'I could contain myself no longer: "Wretch!" I exclaimed,
"dost thou imagine that my father's heart could brook dependence on the destroyer of his child, and tamely accept of a base
equivalent for her honour and his own!" "Honour, my Emily,"
said he, "is the word of fools, or of those wiser men who cheat
them. 'Tis a fantastic bauble that does not suit the gravity of your

father's age; but, whatever it is, I am afraid it can never be perfectly restored to you: exchange the word then, and let pleasure be your object now." At these words he clasped me in his arms, and pressed his lips rudely to my bosom. I started from my seat, "Perfidious villain!" said I, "who dar'st insult the weakness thou hast undone; were that father here, thy coward-soul would shrink from the vengeance of his honour! Curst be that wretch who has deprived him of it! oh! doubly curst, who has dragg'd on his hoary head the infamy which should have crushed her own!" I snatched a knife which lay beside me, and would have plunged it in my breast; but the monster prevented my purpose, and smiling with the grin of barbarous insult, "Madam," said he, "I confess you are rather too much in heroics for me: I am sorry we should differ about trifles; but as I seem somehow to have offended you, I would willingly remedy it by taking my leave. You have been put to some foolish expence in this journey on my account; allow me to reimburse you." So saying, he laid a bank-bill, of what amount I had no patience to see, upon the table. Shame, grief, and indignation, choaked my utterance; unable to speak my wrongs, and unable to bear them in silence, I fell in a swoon at his feet.

'What happened in the interval I cannot tell; but when I came to myself, I was in the arms of the land-lady, with her niece chafing my temples, and doing all in her power for my recovery. She had much compassion in her countenance: the old woman assumed the softest look she was capable of, and both endeavoured to bring me comfort. They continued to show me many civilities, and even the aunt began to be less disagreeable in my sight. To the wretched, to the forlorn, as I was, small offices of kindness are endearing.

'Mean time my money was far spent, nor did I attempt to conceal my wants from their knowledge. I had frequent thoughts of returning to my father; but the dread of a life of scorn is insurmountable. I avoided therefore going abroad when I had a chance of being seen by any former acquaintance, nor indeed did my health for a great while permit it; and suffered the old woman, at her own suggestion, to call me niece at home, where we now and then saw (when they could prevail on me to leave my room) one or two other elderly women and sometimes a grave business-like man, who showed great compassion for my indisposition, and made me very obligingly an offer of a room at his country-house for the recovery of my health. This offer I did not chuse to accept; but told my landlady, "that I should be glad to be employed in any way of business which my skill in needle-work could recommend me to; confessing, at the same time, that I was afraid I should scarce be able to pay her what I already owed for board and lodging, and that for her other good offices, I had nothing but thanks to give her."

'"My dear child," said she, "do not talk of paying; since I lost my own sweet girl," (here she wept) "your very picture she was, Miss Emily, I have no body, except my niece, to whom I should leave any little thing I have been able to save: you shall live with me, my dear; and I have sometimes a little millenery work,* in which, when you are inclined to it, you may assist us. By the way, here are a pair of ruffles we have just finished for that gentleman you saw here at tea; a distant relation of mine, and a worthy man he is. 'Twas pity you refused the offer of an apartment at his country-house; my niece, you know, was to have accompanied you, and you might have fancied yourself at home: a most sweet place it is, and but a short mile beyond Hampstead. Who knows, Miss Emily, what effects such a visit might have had: if I had half your beauty, I should not waste it pining after e'er a worthless fellow of them all." I felt my heart swell at her words; I would have been angry if I could; but I was in that stupid state which is not easily awakened to anger: when I would have chid her, the reproof stuck in my throat; I could only weep!

'Her want of respect increased, as I had not spirit to assert it; my work was now rather imposed than offered, and I became a drudge for the bread I eat: but my dependance and servility grew in proportion, and I was now in a situation which could not make any extraordinary exertions to disengage itself from either; I found myself with child.

'At last the wretch, who had thus trained me to destruction, hinted the purpose for which those means had been used. I discovered her to be an artful procuress for the pleasures of those, who are men of decency to the world in the midst of debauchery.

'I roused every spark of courage within me at the horrid proposal. She treated my passion at first somewhat mildly; but when I continued to exert it, she resented it with insult, and told me plainly, That if I did not soon comply with her desires, I should pay her every farthing I owed, or rot in a jail for life. I trembled at the thought; still, however, I resisted her importunities, and she put her threats in execution. I was conveyed to prison, weak from my condition, weaker from that struggle of grief and misery which for some time I had suffered. A miscarriage was the consequence.

'Amidst all the horrors of such a state, surrounded with wretches totally callous, lost alike to humanity and to shame, think, Mr. Harley, think what I endured: nor wonder that I at last yielded to the solicitations of that miscreant I had seen at her house, and sunk to the prostitution which he tempted. But that was happiness compared to what I have suffered since. He soon abandoned me to the common use of the town, and I was cast among those miserable beings in whose society I have since remained.

'Oh! did the daughters of virtue know our sufferings! did they see our hearts torn with anguish amidst the affectation of gaiety which our faces are obliged to assume; our bodies tortured by disease, our minds with that consciousness which they cannot lose! Did they know, did they think of this, Mr. Harley!—their censures are just; but their pity perhaps might spare the wretches whom their justice should condemn.

'Last night, but for an exertion of benevolence which the infection of our infamy prevents even in the humane, had I been thrust out from this miserable place which misfortune has yet left me; exposed to the brutal insults of drunkenness, or dragged by that justice which I could not bribe, to the punishment which may correct, but, alas! can never amend the abandoned objects of its terrors. From that, Mr. Harley, your goodness has relieved me.'

He beckoned with his hand: he would have stopped the mention of his favours; but he could not speak, had it been to beg a diadem.

She saw his tears; her fortitude began to fail at the sight, when the voice of some stranger on the stairs awakened her attention. She listened for a moment; then starting up, exclaimed, 'Merciful God! my father's voice!'

She had scarce uttered the word, when the door burst open, and a man entered in the garb of an officer. When he discovered his daughter and Harley, he started back a few paces; his look assumed a furious wildness! he laid his hand on his sword. The two objects of his wrath did not utter a syllable. 'Villain,' he cried, 'thou seest a father who had once a daughter's honour to preserve; blasted as it now is, behold him ready to avenge its loss!'

Harley had by this time some power of utterance. 'Sir,' said he, 'if you will be a moment calm'—'Infamous coward!' interrupted the other, 'dost thou preach calmness to wrongs like mine?' He drew his sword. 'Sir,' said Harley, 'let me tell you'—The blood ran quicker to his cheek—his pulse beat one—no more—and regained the temperament of humanity!—'You are deceived, Sir,' said he, 'you are much deceived; but I forgive suspicions which you misfortunes have justified: I would not wrong you, upon my soul, I would not, for the dearest gratification of a thousand worlds: my heart bleeds for you!'

His daughter was now prostrate at his feet. 'Strike,' said she, 'strike here a wretch, whose misery cannot end but with that death she deserves.' Her hair had fallen on her shoulders! her look had the horrid calmness of outbreathed despair! Her father would have spoken; his lip quivered, his cheek grew pale! his eyes lost the lightening of their fury! there was a reproach in them, but with a mingling of pity! He turned them up to heaven—then on his daughter.—He laid his left hand on his heart—the sword dropped from his right—he burst into tears.

CHAPTER XXIX

THE DISTRESSES OF A FATHER

HARLEY kneeled also at the side of the unfortunate daughter: 'Allow me, Sir,' said he, 'to intreat your pardon for one whose offences have been already so signally punished. I know, I feel, that those tears, wrung from the heart of a father, are more dreadful to her than all the punishments your sword could have inflicted: accept the contrition of a child whom heaven has restored to you.' 'Is she not lost,' answered he, 'irrecoverably lost? Damnation! a common prostitute to the meanest ruffian!'—'Calmly, my dear Sir,' said Harley, 'did you know by what complicated misfortunes she had fallen to that miserable state in which you now behold her, I should have no need of words to excite your compassion. Think, Sir, of what once she was! Would you abandon her to the insults of an unfeeling world, deny her opportunity of penitence, and cut off the little comfort that still remains for your afflictions and her own!' 'Speak,' said he, addressing himself to his daughter; 'speak, I will hear thee.'—The desperation that supported her was lost; she fell to the ground, and bathed his feet with her tears!— NT allusion

Harley undertook her cause: he related the treacheries to which she had fallen a sacrifice, and again solicited the forgiveness of her father. He looked on her for some time in silence; the pride of a soldier's honour checked for a while the yearnings of his heart; but nature at last prevailed, he fell on her neck, and mingled his tears with hers.

Harley, who discovered from the dress of the stranger that he was just arrived from a journey, begged that they would both remove to his lodgings, till he could procure others for them. Atkins looked at him with some marks of surprise. His daughter now first recovered the power of speech: 'Wretch as I am,' said she, 'yet there is some gratitude due to the preserver of your child. See him now before you. To him I owe my life, or at least the comfort of imploring your forgiveness before I die.' 'Pardon me, young gentleman,' said Atkins, 'I fear my passion wronged you.'

'Never, never, Sir,' said Harley; 'if it had, your reconciliation to your daughter were an atonement a thousand fold.' He then repeated his request that he might be allowed to conduct them to his lodgings, to which Mr. Atkins at last consented. He took his daughter's arm, 'Come, my Emily,' said he, 'we can never, never recover that happiness we have lost; but time may teach us to remember our misfortunes with patience.'

When they arrived at the house where Harley lodged, he was informed, that the first floor was then vacant, and that the gentleman and his daughter might be accommodated there. While he was upon this inquiry, Miss Atkins informed her father more particularly what she owed to his benevolence. When he returned into the room where they were, Atkins ran and embraced him; begged him again to forgive the offence he had given him, and made the warmest protestations of gratitude for his favours. We would attempt to describe the joy which Harley felt on this occasion, did it not occur to us, that one half of the world could not understand it though we did; and the other half will, by this time, have understood it without any description at all.

Miss Atkins now retired to her chamber, to take some rest from the violence of the emotions she had suffered. When she was gone, her father, addressing himself to Harley, said, 'You have a right, Sir, to be informed of the present situation of one who owes so much to your compassion for his misfortunes. My daughter I find has informed you what that was at the fatal juncture when they began. Her distresses you have heard, you have pitied as they deserved; with mine perhaps I cannot so easily make you acquainted. You have a feeling heart, Mr. Harley; I bless it that it has saved my child; but you never were a father; a father, torn by that most dreadful of calamities, the dishonour of a child he doated on! You have been already informed of some of the circumstances of her elopement. I was then from home, called by the death of a relation, who, though he would never advance me a shilling on the utmost exigency in his lifetime, left me all the gleanings of his frugality at his death. I would not write this intelligence to my daughter, because I intended to be the bearer myself; and as soon as my business would allow me, I set out on my return, winged with all the haste of paternal affection. I fondly built those schemes of future happiness, which present prosperity is ever busy to suggest: my Emily was concerned in them all. As I approached our little dwelling, my heart throbbed with the anticipation of joy and welcome. I imagined the cheering fire, the blissful contentment of a frugal meal, made luxurious by a daughter's smile: I painted to myself her surprize at the tidings of our new-acquired riches, our fond disputes about the disposal of them.

'The road was shortened by the dreams of happiness I enjoyed, and it began to be dark as I reached the house: I alighted from my horse, and walked softly up stairs to the room we commonly sat in. I was somewhat disappointed at not finding my daughter there. I rung the bell; her maid appeared, and showed no small signs of wonder at the summons. She blessed herself as she entered the room: I smiled at her surprize. "Where is Miss Emily, Sir?" said she. "Emily!" "Yes, Sir; she has been gone hence some days, upon receipt of those letters you sent her." "Letters!" said I. "Yes, Sir; so she told me, and went off in all haste that very night."

'I stood aghast as she spoke; but was able so far to recollect myself, as to put on the affectation of calmness, and telling her there was certainly some mistake in the affair, desired her to leave me.

'When she was gone, I threw myself into a chair in that state of uncertainty which is of all others the most dreadful. The gay visions with which I had delighted myself, vanished in an instant: I was tortured with tracing back the same circle of doubt and disappointment. My head grew dizzy as I thought: I called the servant again, and asked her a hundred questions to no purpose; there was not room even for conjecture.

'Something at last arose in my mind, which we call Hope, without knowing what it is. I wished myself deluded by it; but it could not prevail over my returning fears. I rose and walked through the room. My Emily's spinet stood at the end of it, open, with a book of music folded down at some of my favourite lessons. I touched the keys; there was a vibration in the sound that froze my blood: I looked around, and methought the family-pictures on the walls gazed on me with compassion in their faces. I sat down again with an attempt at more composure; I started at every creaking of the door, and my ears rung with imaginary noises!

'I had not remained long in this situation, when the arrival of a friend, who had accidentally heard of my return, put an end to my doubts, by the recital of my daughter's dishonour. He told me he had his information from a young gentleman, to whom Winbrooke had boasted of having seduced her.

'I started from my seat, with broken curses on my lips, and, without knowing whither I should pursue them, ordered my servant to load my pistols, and saddle my horses. My friend, however, with great difficulty, persuaded me to compose myself for that night, promising to accompany me on the morrow to Sir George Winbrooke's in quest of his son.

'The morrow came, after a night spent in a state little distant from madness. We went as early as decency would allow to Sir George's; he received me with politeness, and indeed compassion; protested his abhorrence of his son's conduct, and told me that he had set out some days before for London, on which place he had procured a draught for a large sum, on pretence of finishing his travels; but that he had not heard from him since his departure.

'I did not wait for any more, either of information or comfort; but, against the united remonstrances of Sir George and my friend, set out instantly for London with a frantic uncertainty of purpose; but there all manner of search was in vain. I could trace neither of them any farther than the inn where they first put up on their arrival; and after some days fruitless inquiry, returned home destitute of every little hope that had hitherto supported me. The journeys I had made, the restless nights I had spent, above all, the perturbation of my mind, had the effect which naturally might be expected; a very dangerous fever was the consequence. From this, however, contrary to the expectation of my physicians, I recovered. It was now that I first felt something like calmness of mind; probably from being reduced to a state which could not produce the exertions of anguish or despair. A stupid melancholy settled on my soul: I could endure to live with an apathy of life; at times I forgot my resentment, and wept at the remembrance of my child.

'Such has been the tenor of my days since that fatal moment when these misfortunes began, till yesterday, that I received a letter from a friend in town, acquainting me of her present situation. Could such tales as mine, Mr. Harley, be sometimes suggested to the daughters of levity, did they but know with what anxiety the heart of a parent flutters round the child he loves, they would be less apt to construe into harshness that delicate concern for their conduct, which they often complain of as laying restraint upon things, to the young, the gay, and the thoughtless, seemingly harmless and indifferent. Alas! I fondly imagined that I needed not even these common cautions! my Emily was the joy of my age, and the pride of my soul!—Those things are now no more! they are lost for ever! Her death I could have born! but the death of her honour has added obloquy and shame to that sorrow which bends my gray hairs to the dust!'

As he spoke these last words, his voice trembled in his throat; it was now lost in his tears! He sat with his face half turned from Harley, as if he would have hid the sorrow which he felt. Harley was in the same attitude himself; he durst not meet his eye with a tear; but gathering his stifled breath, 'Let me intreat you, Sir,' said he, 'to hope better things. The world is ever tyrannical; it warps our sorrows to edge them with keener affliction: let us not be slaves to the names it affixes to motive or to action. I know an ingenuous mind cannot help feeling when they sting: but there are considerations by which it may be overcome; its fantastic ideas vanish as they rise; they teach us—to look beyond it.'

*   *   *   *   *

A FRAGMENT

SHOWING HIS SUCCESS WITH THE BARONET

* 　* 　* 　THE card he received was in the politest style in which disappointment could be communicated; the baronet 'was under a necessity of giving up his application for Mr. Harley, as he was informed, that the lease was engaged for a gentleman who had long served his majesty in another capacity, and whose merit had entitled him to the first lucrative thing that should be vacant.' Even Harley could not murmur at such a disposal.—'Perhaps,' said he to himself, 'some war-worn officer, who, like poor Atkins, had been neglected from reasons which merited the highest advancement; whose honour could not stoop to solicit the preferment he deserved; perhaps, with a family, taught the principles of delicacy, without the means of supporting it; a wife and children—gracious heaven! whom my wishes would have deprived of bread.'—

He was interrupted in his reverie by some one tapping him on the shoulder, and, on turning round, he discovered it to be the very man who had explained to him the condition of his gay companion at Hydepark-corner. 'I am glad to see you, Sir,' said he; 'I believe we are fellows in disappointment.' Harley stared, and said that he was at a loss to understand him. 'Poh! you need not be so shy,' answered the other; 'every one for himself is but fair, and I had much rather you had got it than the rascally gauger.' Harley still protested his ignorance of what he meant. 'Why, the lease of Bancroft-manor; had not you been applying for it?' 'I confess I was,' replied Harley; 'but I cannot conceive how you should be interested in the matter.'—'Why, I was making interest for it myself,' said he, 'and I think I had some title: I voted for this same baronet at the last election, and made some of my friends do so too; though I would not have you imagine that I sold my vote; no, I scorn it, let me tell you, I scorn it; but I thought as how this man was staunch and true, and I find he's but a double-faced fellow after all, and speechifies in the house for any side he hopes to make most by. Oh! how many fine speeches and squeezings by the hand we had of him on the canvass! "And if I shall ever be so happy as to have an opportunity of serving you"—A murrain* on the smooth-tongu'd knave; and after all to get it for this pimp of a gauger.'——'The gauger! there must be some mistake,' said Harley; 'he writes me, that it was engaged for one whose long services'—'Services!' interrupted the other; 'you shall hear: Services! Yes, his sister arrived in town a few days ago, and is now sempstress to the baronet. A plague on all rogues! says honest Sam Wrightson; I shall but just drink damnation to them to-night, in a crown's-worth of Ashley's, and leave London to-morrow by sun-rise.'—'I shall leave it too,' said Harley; and so he accordingly did.

In passing through Piccadilly, he had observed on the window of an inn a notification of the departure of a stage-coach for a place in his road homewards; in the way back to his lodgings he took a seat in it for his return.

CHAPTER XXXIII

HE LEAVES LONDON—CHARACTERS IN A STAGE-COACH

THE company in the stage-coach consisted of a grocer and his wife, who were going to pay a visit to some of their country friends; a young officer, who took this way of marching to quarters; a middle-aged gentlewoman, who had been hired as housekeeper to some family in the country; and an elderly well-looking man, with a remarkable old-fashioned periwig.

Harley, upon entering, discovered but one vacant seat, next the grocer's wife, which, from his natural shyness of temper, he made no scruple to occupy, however aware that riding backwards always disagreed with him.

Though his inclination to physiognomy had met with some rubs in the metropolis, he had not yet lost his attachment to that science: he set himself therefore to examine, as usual, the countenances of his companions. Here indeed he was not long in doubt as to the preference; for besides that the elderly gentleman, who sat opposite to him, had features by nature more expressive of good dispositions, there was something in that periwig we mentioned peculiarly attractive of Harley's regard.

He had not been long employed in these speculations, when he found himself attacked with that faintish sickness, which was the natural consequence of his situation in the coach. The paleness of his countenance was first observed by the housekeeper, who immediately made offer of her smelling-bottle, which Harley however declined, telling at the same time the cause of his uneasiness. The gentleman on the opposite side of the coach now first turned his eye from the side-direction in which it had been fixed, and begged Harley to exchange places with him, expressing his regret that he had not made the proposal before. Harley thanked him; and, upon being assured that both seats were alike to him, was about to accept of his offer, when the young gentleman of the sword, putting on an arch look, laid hold of the other's arm, 'So, my old boy,' said he, 'I find you have still some youthful blood about you; but, with your leave, I will do myself the honour of sitting by this lady;' and took his place accordingly. The grocer stared him as full in the face as his own short neck would allow; and his wife, who was a little round-fac'd woman, with a great deal of colour in her cheeks, drew up at the compliment that was paid her, looking first at the officer, and then at the housekeeper.

This incident was productive of some discourse; for before, though there was sometimes a cough or a hem from the grocer, and the officer now and then humm'd a few notes of a song, there had not a single word passed the lips of any of the company.

Mrs. Grocer observed, how ill-convenient it was for people, who could not be drove backwards, to travel in a stage. This brought on a dissertation on stage-coaches in general, and the pleasure of keeping a chay* of one's own; which led to another, on the great riches of Mr. Deputy Bearskin, who, according to her, had once been of that industrious order of youths who sweep the crossings of the streets for the conveniency of passengers, but, by various fortunate accidents, had now acquired an immense fortune, and kept his coach and a dozen livery servants. All this afforded ample fund for conversation, if conversation it might be called, that was carried on solely by the before-mentioned lady, nobody offering to interrupt her, except that the officer sometimes signified his approbation by a variety of oaths, a sort of phraseology in which he seemed extremely versant. She appealed indeed frequently to her husband for the authenticity of certain facts, of which the good man as often protested his total ignorance; but as he was always called fool, or something very like it, for his pains, he at last contrived to support the credit of his wife without prejudice to his conscience, and signified his assent by a noise not unlike the grunting of that animal which in shape and fatness he somewhat resembled.

The housekeeper, and the old gentleman who sat next to Harley, were now observed to be fast asleep; at which the lady, who had been at such pains to entertain them, muttered some words of displeasure, and, upon the officer's whispering to smoke the old put,* both she and her husband purs'd up their mouths into a contemptuous smile. Harley looked sternly on the grocer: 'You are come, Sir,' said he, 'to those years when you might have learned some reverence for age: as for this young man, who has so lately escaped from the nursery, he may be allowed to divert himself.' 'Dam'-me, Sir,' said the officer, 'do you call me young?' striking up the front of his hat, and stretching forward on his seat, till his face almost touched Harley's. It is probable, however, that he discovered something there which tended to pacify him; for, on the lady's intreating them not to quarrel, he very soon resumed his posture and calmness together, and was rather less profuse of his oaths during the rest of the journey.

It is possible the old gentleman had waked time enough to hear the last part of this discourse; at least (whether from that cause, or that he too was a physiognomist) he wore a look remarkably complacent* to Harley, who, on his part, shewed a particular observance of him: indeed they had soon a better opportunity of making their acquaintance, as the coach arrived that night at the town where the officer's regiment lay, and the places of destination of their other fellow-travellers, it seems, were at no great distance; for next morning the old gentleman and Harley were the only passengers remaining.

When they left the inn in the morning, Harley, pulling out a little pocket-book, began to examine the contents, and make some corrections with a pencil. 'This,' said he, turning to his companion, 'is an amusement with which I sometimes pass idle hours at an inn: these are quotations from those humble poets, who trust their fame to the brittle tenure of windows and drinking-glasses.' 'From our inns,' returned the gentleman, 'a stranger might imagine that we were a nation of poets; machines at least containing poetry, which the notion of a journey emptied of their contents: is it from the vanity of being thought geniuses, or a mere mechanical imitation of the custom of others, that we are tempted to scrawl rhime upon such places?'

'Whether vanity is the cause of our becoming rhimesters or not,' answered Harley, 'it is a pretty certain effect of it. An old man of my acquaintance, who deals in apothegms, used to say, That he had known few men without envy, few wits without ill-nature, and no poet without vanity; and I believe his remark is a pretty just one: vanity has been immemorially the charter of poets. In this the ancients were more honest than we are; the old poets frequently make boastful predictions of the immortality their works shall acquire them; ours, in their dedications and prefatory discourses, employ much eloquence to praise their patrons, and much seeming modesty to condemn themselves, or at least to apologize for their productions to the world: but this, in my opinion, is the more assuming manner of the two; for of all the garbs I ever saw pride put on, that of her humility is to me the most disgusting.'

'It is natural enough for a poet to be vain,' said the stranger: 'the little worlds which he raises, the inspiration which he claims, may easily be productive of self-importance; though that inspiration is fabulous, it brings on egotism, which is always the parent of vanity.'

'It may be supposed,' answered Harley, 'that inspiration of old was an article of religious faith; in modern times it may be translated a propensity to compose; and I believe it is not always most readily found where the poets have fixed its residence, amidst groves and plains, and the scenes of pastoral retirement. The mind may be there unbent from the cares of the world; but it will frequently, at the same time, be unnerved from any great exertion: it will feel imperfect ideas which it cannot express, and wander without effort over the regions of reflection.'

'There is at least,' said the stranger, 'one advantage in the poetical inclination, that it is an incentive to philanthropy. There is a certain poetic ground, on which a man cannot tread without feelings that enlarge the heart: the causes of human depravity vanish before the romantic enthusiasm he professes; and many who are not able to reach the Parnassian heights, may yet approach so near as to be bettered by the air of the climate.'

'I have always thought so,' replied Harley; 'but this is an argument with the prudent against it: they urge the danger of unfitness for the world.' — *Johnson*

'I allow it,' returned the other; 'but I believe it is not always rightfully imputed to the bent for poetry: that is only one effect of the common cause.—Jack, says his father, is indeed no scholar; nor could all the drubbings from his master ever bring him one step forward in his accidence or syntax: but I intend him for a merchant.—Allow the same indulgence to Tom.—Tom reads Virgil and Horace when he should be casting accounts; and but t'other day he pawned his great-coat for an edition of Shakespeare.—But Tom would have been as he is, though Virgil and Horace had never been born, though Shakespeare had died a link-boy,* for his nurse will tell you, that when he was a child, he broke his rattle, to discover what it was that sounded within it; and burnt the sticks of his go-cart, because he liked to see the sparkling of timber in the fire.—'Tis a sad case; but what is to be done?—Why, Jack shall make a fortune, dine on venison, and drink claret.—Ay, but Tom—Tom shall dine with his brother, when his pride will let him; at other times, he shall bless God over a half-pint of ale and a Welsh-rabbit; and both shall go to heaven as they may.—That's a poor prospect for Tom, says the father.— To go to heaven! I cannot agree with him.'

'Perhaps,' said Harley, 'we now-a-days discourage the romantic turn a little too much. Our boys are prudent too soon. Mistake me not, I do not mean to blame them for want of levity or dissipation; but their pleasures are those of hackneyed vice, blunted to every finer emotion by the repetition of debauch; and their desire of pleasure is warped to the desire of wealth, as the means of procuring it. The immense riches acquired by individuals have erected a standard of ambition, destructive of private morals, and of public virtue. The weaknesses of vice are left us; but the most allowable of our failings we are taught to despise. Love, the passion most natural to the sensibility of youth, has lost the plaintive dignity he once possessed, for the unmeaning simper of a dangling coxcomb; and the only serious concern, that of a dowry, is settled, even amongst the beardless leaders of the dancing-school. The Frivolous and the Interested (might a satyrist say) are the characteristical features of the age; they are visible even in the essays of our philosophers. They laugh at the pedantry of our fathers, who complained of the times in which they lived; they are at pains to persuade us how much those were deceived; they pride themselves in defending things as they find them, and in exploring the barren sounds which had been reared into motives for action. To this their style is suited; and the manly tone of reason is exchanged for perpetual efforts at sneer and ridicule. This I hold to be an alarming crisis in the corruption of a state; when not only is virtue declined, and vice prevailing, but when the praises of virtue are forgotten, and the infamy of vice unfelt.'

They soon after arrived at the next inn upon the route of the stage-coach, when the stranger told Harley, that his brother's house, to which he was returning, lay at no great distance, and he must therefore unwillingly bid him adieu.

'I should like,' said Harley, taking his hand, 'to have some word to remember so much seeming worth by: my name is Harley.'—'I shall remember it,' answered the old gentleman, 'in my prayers; mine is Silton.'

And Silton indeed it was; Ben Silton himself! Once more, my honoured friend, farewel!——Born to be happy without the world, to that peaceful happiness which the world has not to bestow! Envy never scowled on thy life, nor hatred smiled on thy grave.

CHAPTER XXXIV

HE MEETS AN OLD ACQUAINTANCE

WHEN the stage-coach arrived at the place of its destination, Harley began to consider how he should proceed the remaining part of his journey. He was very civilly accosted by the master of the inn, who offered to accommodate him either with a post-chaise or horses, to any distance he had a mind: but as he did things frequently in a way different from what other people call natural, he refused these offers, and set out immediately a-foot, having first put a spare shirt in his pocket, and given directions for the forwarding of his portmanteau. This was a method of travelling which he was accustomed to take; it saved the trouble of provision for any animal but himself, and left him at liberty to chuse his quarters, either at an inn, or at the first cottage in which he saw a face he liked: nay, when he was not peculiarly attracted by the reasonable creation, he would sometimes consort with a species of inferior rank, and lay himself down to sleep by the side of a rock, or on the banks of a rivulet. He did few things without a motive, but his motives were rather eccentric; and the useful and expedient were terms which he held to be very indefinite, and which therefore he did not always apply to the sense in which they are commonly understood.

The sun was now in his decline, and the evening remarkably serene, when he entered a hollow part of the road, which winded between the surrounding banks, and seamed the sward in different lines, as the choice of travellers had directed them to tread it. It seemed to be little frequented now, for some of those had partly recovered their former verdure. The scene was such as induced Harley to stand and enjoy it; when, turning round, his notice was attracted by an object, which the fixture of his eye on the spot he walked had before prevented him from observing.

An old man, who from his dress seemed to have been a soldier, lay fast asleep on the ground; a knapsack rested on a stone at his right hand, while his staff and brass-hilted sword were crossed at his left.

Harley looked on him with the most earnest attention. He was one of those figures which Salvator* would have drawn; nor was the surrounding scenery unlike the wildness of that painter's backgrounds. The banks on each side were covered with fantastic shrub-wood, and at a little distance, on the top of one of them, stood a finger-post, to mark the directions of two roads which diverged from the point where it was placed. A rock, with some dangling wild flowers, jutted out above where the soldier lay; on which grew the stump of a large tree, white with age, and a single twisted branch shaded his face as he slept. His face had the marks of manly comeliness impaired by time; his forehead was not altogether bald, but its hairs might have been numbered; while a few white locks behind crossed the brown of his neck with a contrast the most venerable to a mind like Harley's. 'Thou art old,' said he to himself, 'but age has not brought thee rest for its infirmities; I fear those silver hairs have not found shelter from thy country, though that neck has been bronzed in its service.' The stranger waked. He looked at Harley with the appearance of some confusion: it was a pain the latter knew too well to think of causing in another; he turned and went on. The old man readjusted his knapsack, and followed in one of the tracks on the opposite side of the road.

When Harley heard the tread of his feet behind him, he could not help stealing back a glance at his fellow-traveller. He seemed to bend under the weight of his knapsack; he halted on his walk, and one of his arms was supported by a sling, and lay motionless across his breast. He had that steady look of sorrow, which indicates that its owner has gazed upon his griefs till he has forgotten to lament them; yet not without those streaks of complacency, which a good mind will sometimes throw into the countenance, through all the incumbent load of its depression.

He had now advanced nearer to Harley, and, with an uncertain sort of voice, begged to know what it was o'clock; 'I fear,' said he, 'sleep has beguiled me of my time, and I shall hardly have light enough left to carry me to the end of my journey.' 'Father!' said

Harley, (who by this time found the romantic enthusiasm rising within him) 'how far do you mean to go?' 'But a little way, Sir,' returned the other; 'and indeed it is but a little way I can manage now: 'tis just four miles from the height to the village, thither I am going.' 'I am going there too,' said Harley; 'we may make the road shorter to each other. You seem to have served your country, Sir, to have served it hardly too; 'tis a character I have the highest esteem for.—I would not be impertinently inquisitive; but there is that in your appearance which excites my curiosity to know something more of you: in the mean time suffer me to carry that knapsack.'

The old man gazed on him; a tear stood in his eye! 'Young gentleman,' said he, 'you are too good: may heaven bless you for an old man's sake, who has nothing but his blessing to give! but my knapsack is so familiar to my shoulders, that I should walk the worse for wanting it; and it would be troublesome to you, who have not been used to its weight.' 'Far from it,' answered Harley, 'I should tread the lighter; it would be the most honourable badge I ever wore.'

'Sir,' said the stranger, who had looked earnestly in Harley's face during the last part of his discourse, 'is not your name Harley?' 'It is,' replied he; 'I am ashamed to say I have forgotten yours.' 'You may well have forgotten my face,' said the stranger, ''tis a long time since you saw it; but possibly you may remember something of old Edwards.'—'Edwards!' cried Harley, 'Oh! heavens!' and sprung to embrace him; 'let me clasp those knees on which I have sat so often: Edwards!——I shall never forget that fire-side, round which I have been so happy! But where, where have you been? where is Jack? where is your daughter? How has it fared with them when fortune, I fear, has been so unkind to you?'—''Tis a long tale,' replied Edwards; 'but I will try to tell it you as we walk.'*

'When you were at school in the neighbourhood, you remember me at South-hill: that farm had been possessed by my father, grandfather, and great-grandfather, which last was a younger brother of that very man's ancestor who is now lord of the manor. I thought I managed it, as they had done, with prudence;

I paid my rent regularly as it became due, and had always as much behind as gave bread to me and my children. But my last lease was out soon after you left that part of the country; and the squire, who had lately got a London-attorney for his steward, would not renew it, because, he said, he did not chuse to have any farm under 300 l. a year value on his estate; but offered to give me the preference on the same terms with another, if I chose to take the one he had marked out, of which mine was a part.

'What could I do, Mr. Harley? I feared the undertaking was too great for me; yet to leave, at my age, the house I had lived in from my cradle! I could not, Mr. Harley, I could not; there was not a tree about it that I did not look on as my father, my brother, or my child: so I even ran the risk, and took the squire's offer of the whole. But I had soon reason to repent of my bargain: the steward had taken care that my former farm should be the best land of the division: I was obliged to hire more servants, and I could not have my eye over them all; some unfavourable seasons followed one another, and I found my affairs entangling on my hands. To add to my distress, a considerable corn-factor turned bankrupt with a sum of mine in his possession: I failed paying my rent so punctually as I was wont to do, and the same steward had my stock taken in execution in a few days after. So, Mr. Harley, there was an end of my prosperity. However, there was as much produced from the sale of my effects as paid my debts and saved me from a jail: I thank God I wronged no man, and the world could never charge me with dishonesty.

'Had you seen us, Mr. Harley, when we were turned out of South-hill, I am sure you would have wept at the sight. You remember old Trusty, my shag house-dog; I shall never forget it while I live; the poor creature was blind with age, and could scarce crawl after us to the door; he went however as far as the gooseberry-bush; that you may remember stood on the left side of the yard; he was wont to bask in the sun there: when he had reached that spot, he stopped; we went on: I called to him; he wagged his tail, but did not stir: I called again; he lay down: I whistled, and cried "Trusty"; he gave a short howl, and died!

alludes to the
Odyssey

I could have lain down and died too; but God gave me strength to live for my children.'

The old man now paused a moment to take breath. He eyed Harley's face; it was bathed in tears: the story was grown familiar to himself; he dropped one tear and no more.

'Though I was poor,' continued he, 'I was not altogether without credit. A gentleman in the neighbourhood, who had a small farm unoccupied at the time, offered to let me have it, on giving security for the rent, which I made shift to procure. It was a piece of ground which required management to make any thing of; but it was nearly within the compass of my son's labour and my own. We exerted all our industry to bring it into some heart. We began to succeed tolerably, and lived contented on its produce, when an unlucky accident brought us under the displeasure of a neighbouring justice of the peace, and broke all our family happiness again.

'My son was a remarkable good shooter; he had always kept a pointer on our former farm, and thought no harm in doing so now; when one day, having sprung a covey on our own ground, the dog, of his own accord, followed them into the justice's. My son laid down his gun, and went after his dog to bring him back: the game-keeper, who had marked the birds, came up, and seeing the pointer, shot him just as my son approached. The creature fell; my son ran up to him: he died with a complaining sort of cry at his master's feet. Jack could bear it no longer; but flying at the game-keeper, wrenched his gun out of his hand, and with the butt end of it felled him to the ground.

'He had scarce got home, when a constable came with a warrant, and dragged him to prison; there he lay, for the justices would not take bail, till he was tried at the quarter-sessions for the assault and battery. His fine was hard upon us to pay; we contrived however to live the worse for it, and make up the loss by our frugality: but the justice was not content with that punishment, and soon after had an opportunity of punishing us indeed.

'An officer with press-orders came down to our county, and having met with the justices, agreed that they should pitch on a certain number, who could most easily be spared from the county, of whom he would take care to clear it: my son's name was in the justices' list.

'''Twas on a Christmas eve, and the birth-day too of my son's little boy. The night was piercing cold, and it blew a storm, with showers of hail and snow. We had made up a cheering fire in an inner room; I sat before it in my wicker-chair, blessing Providence, that had still left a shelter for me and my children. My son's two little ones were holding their gambols around us; my heart warmed at the sight; I brought a bottle of my best ale, and all our misfortunes were forgotten.

'It had long been our custom to play a game at blind-man's-buff on that night, and it was not omitted now; so to it we fell, I, and my son, and his wife, the daughter of a neighbouring farmer, who happened to be with us at the time, the two children, and an old maid-servant, that had lived with me from a child. The lot fell on my son to be blindfolded: we had continued some time in our game, when he groped his way into an outer-room in pursuit of some of us, who, he imagined, had taken shelter there; we kept snug in our places, and enjoyed his mistake. He had not been long there, when he was suddenly seized from behind; "I shall have you now," said he, and turned about. "Shall you so, master," answered the ruffian who had laid hold of him; "we shall make you play at another sort of game by and by."'—At these words Harley started with a convulsive sort of motion, and grasping Edwards's sword, drew it half out of the scabbard, with a look of the most frantic wildness. Edwards gently replaced it in its sheath, and went on with his relation.

'On hearing these words in a strange voice, we all rushed out to discover the cause; the room by this time was almost full of the gang. My daughter-in-law fainted at the sight; the maid and I ran to assist her, while my poor son remained motionless, gazing by turns on his children and their mother. We soon recovered her to life, and begged her to retire and wait the issue of the affair; but she flew to her husband, and clung round him in an agony of terror and grief.

'In the gang was one of a smoother aspect, whom, by his dress, we discovered to be a serjeant of foot: he came up to me, and told me, that my son had his choice of the sea or land service, whispering at the same time, that if he chose the land, he might get off, on procuring him another man, and paying a certain sum for his freedom. The money we could just muster up in the house, by the assistance of the maid, who produced, in a green bag, all the little savings of her service; but the man we could not expect to find. My daughter-in-law gazed upon her children with a look of the wildest despair: "My poor infants!" said she, "your father is forced from you; who shall now labour for your bread; or must your mother beg for herself and you?" I prayed her to be patient; but comfort I had none to give her. At last, calling the serjeant aside, I asked him, "If I was too old to be accepted in place of my son?" "Why, I don't know," said he; "you are rather old to be sure, but yet the money may do much." I put the money in his hand; and coming back to my children, "Jack," said I, "you are free; live to give your wife and these little ones bread; I will go, my child, in your stead: I have but little life to lose, and if I staid, should add one to the wretches you left behind." "No," replied my son, "I am not that coward you imagine me; heaven forbid, that my father's grey hairs should be so exposed, while I sat idle at home; I am young, and able to endure much, and God will take care of you and my family." "Jack," said I, "I will put an end to this matter; you have never hitherto disobeyed me; I will not be contradicted in this; stay at home, I charge you, and, for my sake, be kind to my children."

'Our parting, Mr. Harley, I cannot describe to you; it was the first time we ever had parted: the very press-gang could scarce keep from tears; but the serjeant, who had seemed the softest before, was now the least moved of them all. He conducted me to a party of new-raised recruits, who lay at a village in the neighbourhood; and we soon after joined the regiment. I had not been long with it, when we were ordered to the East Indies, where I was soon made a serjeant, and might have picked up some money, if my heart had been as hard as some others were; but my nature was never of that kind, that could think of getting rich at the expence of my conscience.

'Amongst our prisoners was an old Indian, whom some of our

officers supposed to have a treasure hidden somewhere; which is no uncommon practice in that country. They pressed him to discover it. He declared he had none; but that would not satisfy them: so they ordered him to be tied to a stake, and suffer fifty lashes every morning, till he should learn to speak out, as they said. Oh! Mr. Harley, had you seen him, as I did, with his hands bound behind him, suffering in silence, while the big drops trickled down his shrivelled cheeks, and wet his grey beard, which some of the inhuman soldiers plucked in scorn! I could not bear it, I could not for my soul; and one morning, when the rest of the guard were out of the way, I found means to let him escape. I was tried by a court-martial for negligence of my post, and ordered, in compassion of my age, and having got this wound in my arm, and that in my leg, in the service, only to suffer 300 lashes, and be turned out of the regiment; but my sentence was mitigated as to the lashes, and I had only 200. When I had suffered these, I was turned out of the camp, and had betwixt three and four hundred miles to travel before I could reach a sea-port, without guide to conduct me, or money to buy me provisions by the way. I set out however, resolved to walk as far as I could, and then to lay myself down and die. But I had scarce gone a mile, when I was met by the Indian whom I had delivered. He pressed me in his arms, and kissed the marks of the lashes on my back a thousand times: he led me to a little hut, where some friend of his dwelt; and after I was recovered of my wounds, conducted me so far on my journey himself, and sent another Indian to guide me through the rest. When we parted, he pulled out a purse with two hundred pieces of gold in it: "Take this," said he, "my dear preserver, it is all I have been able to procure." I begged him not to bring himself to poverty for my sake, who should probably have no need of it long; but he insisted on my accepting it. He embraced me:—"You are an Englishman," said he, "but the Great Spirit has given you an Indian heart; may he bear up the weight of your old age, and blunt the arrow that brings it rest!" We parted; and not long after I made shift to get my passage to England. 'Tis but about a week since I landed, and I am going to end my days in the arms of my son. This sum may be of use to him and his children; 'tis all the value I put upon it. I thank heaven I never was covetous of wealth; I never had much, but was always so happy as to be content with my little.'

When Edwards had ended his relation Harley stood a while looking at him in silence; at last he pressed him in his arms, and when he had given vent to the fulness of his heart by a shower of tears, 'Edwards,' said he, 'let me hold thee to my bosom; let me imprint the virtue of thy sufferings on my soul. Come, my honoured veteran! let me endeavour to soften the last days of a life, worn out in the service of humanity: call me also thy son, and let me cherish thee as a father.' Edwards, from whom the recollection of his own sufferings had scarce forced a tear, now blubbered like a boy; he could not speak his gratitude, but by some short exclamations of blessings upon Harley.

CHAPTER XXXV

HE MISSES AN OLD ACQUAINTANCE—AN ADVENTURE CONSEQUENT UPON IT

WHEN they had arrived within a little way of the village they journeyed to, Harley stopped short, and looked stedfastly on the mouldering walls of a ruined house that stood on the roadside: 'Oh heavens!' he cried, 'what do I see: silent, unroofed, and desolate! Are all thy gay tenants gone? do I hear their hum no more? Edwards, look there, look there! the scene of my infant joys, my earliest friendships, laid waste and ruinous! That was the very school where I was boarded when you were at South-hill; 'tis but a twelvemonth since I saw it standing, and its benches filled with cherubs: that opposite side of the road was the green on which they sported; see it now ploughed up! I would have given fifty times its value to have saved it from the sacrilege of that plough.'

'Dear Sir,' replied Edwards, 'perhaps they have left it from choice, and may have got another spot as good.' 'They cannot,' said Harley, 'they cannot! I shall never see the sward covered with its daisies, nor pressed by the dance of the dear innocents: I shall

never see that stump decked with the garlands which their little
hands had gathered. These two long stones which now lie at
the foot of it, were once the supports of a hut I myself assisted
to rear: I have sat on the sods within it, when we had spread
our banquet of apples before us, and been more blest——Oh!
Edwards! infinitely more blest than ever I shall be again.'

Just then a woman passed them on the road, and discovered
some signs of wonder at the attitude of Harley, who stood, with
his hands folded together, looking with a moistened eye on the
fallen pillars of the hut. He was too much entranced in thought
to observe her at all; but Edwards civilly accosting her, desired to
know, if that had not been the school-house, and how it came into
the condition in which they now saw it? 'Alack a-day!' said she, 'it
was the school-house indeed; but to be sure, Sir, the squire has
pulled it down, because it stood in the way of his prospects.*—
'What! how! prospects! pulled down!' cried Harley.—'Yes, to be
sure, Sir; and the green, where the children used to play, he has
ploughed up, because, he said, they hurt his fence on the other
side of it.'—'Curses on his narrow heart,' cried Harley, 'that
could violate a right so sacred! Heaven blast the wretch!

> "And from his derogate body never spring
> "A babe to honour him!——*"

But I need not, Edwards, I need not,' (recovering himself a little)
'he is cursed enough already: to him the noblest source of happiness is denied; and the cares of his sordid soul shall gnaw it, while
thou sittest over a brown crust, smiling on those mangled limbs
that have saved thy son and his children!' 'If you want any thing
with the school-mistress, Sir,' said the woman, 'I can show you
the way to her house.' He followed her without knowing whither
he went.

They stopped at the door of a snug habitation, where sat an
elderly woman with a boy and a girl before her, each of whom
held a supper of bread and milk in their hands. 'There, Sir, is the
school-mistress.'—'Madam,' said Harley, 'was not an old venerable man school-master here some time ago?' 'Yes, Sir, he was;
poor man! the loss of his former school-house, I believe, broke his

heart, for he died soon after it was taken down; and as another has not yet been found, I have that charge in the mean time.'—'And this boy and girl, I presume, are your pupils?'—'Ay, Sir, they are poor orphans, put under my care by the parish; and more promising children I never saw.' 'Orphans!' said Harley. 'Yes, Sir, of honest creditable parents as any in the parish; and it is a shame for some folks to forget their relations, at a time when they have most need to remember them.'——'Madam,' said Harley, 'let us never forget that we are all relations.' He kissed the children.

'Their father, Sir,' continued she, 'was a farmer here in the neighbourhood, and a sober industrious man he was; but nobody can help misfortunes: what with bad crops, and bad debts, which are worse, his affairs went to wreck, and both he and his wife died of broken hearts. And a sweet couple they were, Sir; there was not a properer man to look on in the county than John Edwards, and so indeed were all the Edwardses.' 'What Edwardses?' cried the old soldier hastily. 'The Edwardses of South-hill; and a worthy family they were.'——'South-hill!' said he, in languid voice, and fell back into the arms of the astonished Harley. The school-mistress ran for some water, and a smelling-bottle, with the assistance of which they soon recovered the unfortunate Edwards. He stared wildly for some time, then folding his orphan grand-children in his arms, 'Oh! my children, my children!' he cried, 'have I found you thus? My poor Jack! art thou gone? I thought thou shouldst have carried thy father's grey hairs to the grave! And these little ones'—his tears choaked his utterance, and he fell again on the necks of the children.

'My dear old man!' said Harley, 'Providence has sent you to relieve them; it will bless me, if I can be the means of assisting you.'—'Yes indeed, Sir,' answered the boy; 'father, when he was a dying, bade God bless us; and prayed, that if grandfather lived, he might send him to support us.'—'Where did they lay my boy?' said Edwards. 'In the Old Church yard,' replied the woman, 'hard by his mother.'—'I will show it you,' answered the boy; 'for I have wept over it many a time, when first I came amongst strange folks.' He took the old man's hand, Harley laid hold of his sister's, and they walked in silence to the church-yard.

There was an old stone, with the corner broken off, and some letters, half covered with moss, to denote the names of the dead: there was a cyphered R. E. plainer than the rest: it was the tomb they sought. 'Here it is, grandfather,' said the boy. Edwards gazed upon it without uttering a word: the girl, who had only sighed before, now wept outright; her brother sobbed, but he stifled his sobbing. 'I have told sister,' said he, 'that she should not take it so to heart; she can knit already, and I shall soon be able to dig: we shall not starve, sister, indeed we shall not, nor shall grandfather neither.'—The girl cried afresh; Harley kissed off her tears as they flowed, and wept between every kiss.

CHAPTER XXXVI

HE RETURNS HOME—A DESCRIPTION OF HIS RETINUE

IT was with some difficulty that Harley prevailed on the old man to leave the spot where the remains of his son were laid. At last, with the assistance of the school-mistress, he prevailed; and she accommodated Edwards and him with beds in her house, there being nothing like an inn nearer than the distance of some miles.

In the morning, Harley persuaded Edwards to come; with the children, to his house, which was distant but a short day's journey. The boy walked in his grand-father's hand; and the name of Edwards procured him a neighbouring farmer's horse, on which a servant mounted, with the girl on a pillow before him.

With this train Harley returned to the abode of his fathers: and we cannot but think, that his enjoyment was as great as if he had arrived from the tour of Europe, with a Swiss valet for his companion, and half a dozen snuff-boxes, with invisible hinges, in his pocket. But we take our ideas from sounds which folly has invented; Fashion, Bon-ton, and Virtu,* are the names of certain idols, to which we sacrifice the genuine pleasures of the soul: in this world of semblance, we are contented with personating happiness; to feel it, is an art beyond us.

It was otherwise with Harley: he ran up stairs to his aunt, with the history of his fellow-travellers glowing on his lips. His aunt was an economist;* but she knew the pleasure of doing charitable things, and withal was fond of her nephew, and solicitous to oblige him. She received old Edwards therefore with a look of more complacency than is perhaps natural to maiden-ladies of threescore, and was remarkably attentive to his grand-children: she roasted apples with her own hands for their supper, and made up a little bed beside her own for the girl. Edwards made some attempts towards an acknowledgment for these favours; but his young friend stopped them in their beginnings. 'Whosoever receiveth any of these children'—said his aunt; for her acquaintance with her bible was habitual.

Early next morning, Harley stole into the room where Edwards lay: he expected to have found him a-bed; but in this he was mistaken: the old man had risen, and was leaning over his sleeping grand-son, with the tears flowing down his cheeks. At first he did not perceive Harley; when he did, he endeavoured to hide his grief, and crossing his eyes with his hand, expressed his surprise at seeing him so early astir. 'I was thinking of you,' said Harley, 'and your children: I learned last night that a small farm of mine in the neighbourhood is now vacant; if you will occupy it, I shall gain a good neighbour, and be able in some measure to repay the notice you took of me when a boy; and as the furniture of the house is mine, it will be so much trouble saved.' Edwards's tears gushed afresh, and Harley led him to see the place he intended for him.

The house upon this farm was indeed little better than a hut; its situation, however, was pleasant, and Edwards, assisted by the beneficence of Harley, set about improving its neatness and convenience. He staked out a piece of the green before for a garden, and Peter, who acted in Harley's family as valet, butler, and gardener, had orders to furnish him with parcels of the different seeds he chose to sow in it. I have seen his master at work in this little spot, with his coat off, and his dibble* in his hand: it was a scene of tranquil virtue to have stopped an angel on his errands of mercy! Harley had contrived to lead a little bubbling brook through a green walk in the middle of the ground, upon which he had erected a mill in miniature for the diversion of Edwards's infant-grandson, and made shift in its construction to introduce a pliant bit of wood, that answered with its fairy clack to the murmuring of the rill that turned it. I have seen him stand, listening to these mingled sounds, with his eye fixed on the boy, and the smile of conscious satisfaction on his cheek; while the old man, with a look half-turned to Harley, and half to Heaven, breathed an ejaculation of gratitude and piety. — *synonymous*

Father of mercies! I also would thank thee! that not only hast thou assigned eternal rewards to virtue, but that, even in this bad world, the lines of our duty, and our happiness, are so frequently woven together.

A FRAGMENT

THE MAN OF FEELING TALKS OF WHAT HE DOES NOT UNDERSTAND—AN INCIDENT*

* * * * 'EDWARDS,' said he, 'I have a proper regard for the prosperity of my country: every native of it appropriates to himself some share of the power, or the fame, which, as a nation, it acquires; but I cannot throw off the man so much, as to rejoice at our conquests in India. You tell me of immense territories subject to the English: I cannot think of their possessions, without being led to enquire, by what right they possess them. They came there as traders, bartering the commodities they brought for others which their purchasers could spare; and however great their profits were, they were then equitable. But what title have the subjects of another kingdom to establish an empire in India? to give laws to a country where the inhabitants received them on the terms of friendly commerce? You say they are happier under our regulations than the tyranny of their own petty princes. I must doubt it, from the conduct of those by whom these regulations have been made. They have drained the treasuries of Nabobs, who must fill them by oppressing the industry of their subjects. Nor is this to be wondered at, when we consider the motive upon which those gentlemen do not deny their going to India. The fame of conquest, barbarous as that motive is, is but a secondary consideration: there are certain stations in wealth to which the warriors of the East aspire. It is there indeed where the wishes of their friends assign them eminence, where the question of their country is pointed at their return. When shall I see a commander return from India in the pride of honourable poverty?—You describe the victories they have gained; they are sullied by the cause in which they fought: you enumerate the spoils of those victories; they are covered with the blood of the vanquished!

'Could you tell me of some conqueror giving peace and happiness to the conquered? did he accept the gifts of their princes to use them for the comfort of those whose fathers, sons, or husbands, fell in battle? did he use his power to gain security and freedom to the regions of oppression and slavery? did he endear the British name by examples of generosity, which the most barbarous or most depraved are rarely able to resist? did he return with the consciousness of duty discharged to his country, and humanity to his fellow-creatures? did he return with no lace on his coat, no slaves in his retinue, no chariot at his door, and no Burgundy at his table?—these were laurels which princes might envy—which an honest man would not condemn!'

'Your maxims, Mr. Harley, are certainly right,' said Edwards. 'I am not capable of arguing with you; but I imagine there are great temptations in a great degree of riches, which it is no easy matter to resist: those a poor man like me cannot describe, because he never knew them; and perhaps I have reason to bless God that I never did; for then, it is likely, I should have withstood them no better than my neighbours. For you know, Sir, that it is not the fashion now, as it was in former times, that I have read of in books, when your great generals died so poor, that they did not leave wherewithal to buy them a coffin; and people thought the better of their memories for it: if they did so now-a-days, I question if any body, except yourself, and some few like you, would thank them.'

'I am sorry,' replied Harley, 'that there is so much truth in what you say; but however the general current of opinion may point, the feelings are not yet lost that applaud benevolence, and censure inhumanity. Let us endeavour to strengthen them in ourselves; and we, who live sequestered from the noise of the multitude, have better opportunities of listening undisturbed to their voice.'

They now approached the little dwelling of Edwards. A maid-servant, whom he had hired to assist him in the care of his grandchildren, met them a little way from the house: 'There is a young lady within with the children,' said she. Edwards expressed his surprise at the visit: it was however not the less true; and we mean to account for it.

This young lady then was no other than Miss Walton. She had heard the old man's history from Harley, as we have already related it. Curiosity, or some other motive, made her desirous to see his grandchildren: this she had an opportunity of gratifying soon, the children, in some of their walks, having strolled as far as her father's avenue. She put several questions to both; she was delighted with the simplicity of their answers, and promised, that if they continued to be good children, and do as their grandfather bid them, she would soon see them again, and bring some present or other for their reward. This promise she had performed now: she came attended only by her maid, and brought with her a complete suit of green for the boy, and a chintz gown, a cap, and a suit of ribbands, for his sister. She had time enough, with her maid's assistance, to equip them in their new habiliments before Harley and Edwards returned. The boy heard his grandfather's voice, and, with that silent joy which his present finery inspired, ran to the door to meet him: putting one hand in his, with the other pointed to his sister, 'See,' said he, 'what Miss Walton has brought us.'——Edwards gazed on them. Harley fixed his eyes on Miss Walton: hers were turned to the ground;—in Edwards's was a beamy moisture.—He folded his hands together—'I cannot speak, young lady,' said he, 'to thank you.' Neither could Harley. There were a thousand sentiments;—but they gushed so impetuously on his heart, that he could not utter a syllable.*   *   *   *

CHAPTER XL

THE MAN OF FEELING JEALOUS

THE desire of communicating knowledge or intelligence, is an argument with those who hold that man is naturally a social animal. It is indeed one of the earliest propensities we discover; but it may be doubted whether the pleasure (for pleasure there certainly is) arising from it be not often more selfish than social: for we frequently observe the tidings of Ill communicated as eagerly as the annunciation of Good.* Is it that we delight in observing the effects of the stronger passions? for we are all philosophers in this respect; and it is perhaps amongst the spectators at Tyburn* that the most genuine are to be found.

Was it from this motive that Peter came one morning into his master's room with a meaning face of recital? His master indeed did not at first observe it; for he was sitting, with one shoe buckled, delineating portraits in the fire. 'I have brushed those clothes, Sir, as you ordered me.'—Harley nodded his head; but Peter observed that his hat wanted brushing too: his master nodded again. At last Peter bethought him, that the fire needed stirring; and, taking up the poker, demolished the turban'd-head of a Saracen, while his master was seeking out a body for it. 'The morning is main cold, Sir,' said Peter. 'Is it?' said Harley. 'Yes, Sir; I have been as far as Tom Dowson's to fetch some barberries* he had picked for Mrs. Margery. There was a rare junketting last night at Thomas's among Sir Harry Benson's servants: he lay at Squire Walton's, but he would not suffer his servants to trouble the family; so, to be sure, they were all at Tom's, and had a fiddle and a hot supper in the big room where the justices meet about the destroying of hares and partridges, and them things; and Tom's eyes looked so red and so bleared when I called him to get the barberries:—And I hear as how Sir Harry is going to be married to Miss Walton.'—'How! Miss Walton married!' said Harley. 'Why, it mayn't be true, Sir, for all that; but Tom's wife told it me, and to be sure the servants told her, and their master told them, as I guess, Sir; but it mayn't be true

for all that, as I said before.'—'Have done with your idle
information,' said Harley:—'Is my aunt come down into the
parlour to breakfast?'—'Yes, Sir.'—'Tell her I'll be with her
immediately'.——

When Peter was gone, he stood with his eyes fixed on the
ground, and the last words of his intelligence vibrating in his ears.
'Miss Walton married!' he sighed—and walked down stairs, with
his shoe as it was, and the buckle in his hand. His aunt, however,
was pretty well accustomed to those appearances of absence;
besides that, the natural gravity of her temper, which was commonly called into exertion by the care of her household concerns,
was such, as not easily to be discomposed by any circumstance of
accidental impropriety. She too had been informed of the
intended match between Sir Harry Benson and Miss Walton. 'I
have been thinking,' said she, 'that they are distant relations; for
the great-grandfather of this Sir Harry Benson, who was knight
of the shire in the reign of Charles the First and one of the
cavaliers of those times, was married to a daughter of the Walton
family.' Harley answered drily, that it might be so; but that he
never troubled himself about those matters. 'Indeed,' said she,
'you are to blame, nephew, for not knowing a little more of them:
before I was near your age, I had sewed the pedigree of our family
in a set of chair-bottoms, that were made a present of to my
grandmother, who was a very notable woman, and had a proper
regard for gentility, I'll assure you; but now-a-days, it is money,
not birth, that makes people respected; the more shame for the
times.'

Harley was in no very good humour for entering into a discussion of this question; but he always entertained so much filial
respect for his aunt, as to attend to her discourse.

'We blame the pride of the rich,' said he; 'but are not we
ashamed of our poverty?'

'Why, one would not chuse,' replied his aunt, 'to make a much
worse figure than one's neighbours; but, as I was saying before,
the times (as my friend Mrs. Dorothy Walton observes) are
shamefully degenerated in this respect. There was but t'other
day, at Mr. Walton's, that fat fellow's daughter, the London

Merchant,* as he calls himself, though I have heard that he was little better than the keeper of a chandler's shop:—We were leaving the gentlemen to go to tea. She had a hoop forsooth as large and as stiff—and it shewed a pair of bandy legs as thick as two——I was nearer the door by an apron's length, and the pert hussy brushed by me, as who should say, Make way for your betters, and with one of her London-bobs*—but Mrs. Dorothy did not let her pass with it; for all the time of drinking tea, she spoke of the precedency of family, and the disparity there is between people who are come of something, and your mushroom-gentry* who wear their coats of arms in their purses.'

Her indignation was interrupted by the arrival of her maid with a damask table-cloth, and a set of napkins, from the loom, which had been spun by her mistresses own hand. There was the family-crest in each corner, and in the middle a view of the battle of Worcester, where one of her ancestors had been a captain in the king's forces; and, with a sort of poetical licence in perspective, there was seen the Royal Oak,* with more wig than leaves upon it.

On all this the good lady was very copious, and took up the remaining intervals of filling tea, to describe its excellencies to Harley; adding, that she intended this as a present for his wife, when he should get one. He sighed and looked foolish, and commending the serenity of the day, walked out into the garden.

He sat down on a little seat which commanded an extensive prospect round the house. He leaned on his hand, and scored the ground with his stick: 'Miss Walton married!' said he; 'but what is that to me? May she be happy! her virtues deserve it; to me her marriage is otherwise indifferent:—I had romantic dreams! they are fled!—it is perfectly indifferent.'

Just at that moment he saw a servant, with a knot of ribbands in his hat, go into the house. His cheeks grew flushed at the sight! He kept his eye fixed for some time on the door by which he had entered, then starting to his feet, hastily followed him.

When he approached the door of the kitchen where he supposed the man had entered, his heart throbbed so violently, that when he would have called Peter, his voice failed in the attempt.

He stood a moment listening in this breathless state of palpitation: Peter came out by chance. 'Did your honour want any thing?'—'Where is the servant that came just now from Mr. Walton's?'—'From Mr. Walton's, Sir! there is none of his servants here that I know of.'—'Nor of Sir Harry Benson's?'—He did not wait for an answer; but, having by this time observed the hat with its party-coloured ornament hanging on a peg near the door, he pressed forwards into the kitchen and addressing himself to a stranger whom he saw there, asked him, with no small tremor in his voice, If he had any commands for him? The man looked silly, and said, That he had nothing to trouble his honour with. 'Are not you a servant of Sir Harry Benson's?'—'No, Sir.'— 'You'll pardon me, young man; I judged by the favour in your hat.'——'Sir, I'm his majesty's servant, God bless him! and these favours we always wear when we are recruiting.'—'Recruiting!' his eyes glistened at the word: he seized the soldier's hand, and shaking it violently, ordered Peter to fetch a bottle of his aunt's best dram. The bottle was brought: 'You shall drink the king's health,' said Harley, 'in a bumper.'——'The king and your honour.'—'Nay, you shall drink the king's health by itself; you may drink mine in another.' Peter looked in his master's face, and filled with some little reluctance. 'Now to your mistress,' said Harley; 'every soldier has a mistress.' The man excused himself—'to your mistress! you cannot refuse it.' 'Twas Mrs. Margery's best dram! Peter stood with the bottle a little inclined, but not so as to discharge a drop of its contents: 'Fill it, Peter,' said his master, 'fill it to the brim.' Peter filled it; and the soldier having named Suky Simpson, dispatched it in a twinkling. 'Thou art an honest fellow,' said Harley, 'and I love thee;' and shaking his hand again, desired Peter to make him his guest at dinner, and walked up into his room with a pace much quicker and more springy than usual.

This agreeable disappointment however he was not long suffered to enjoy. The curate happened that day to dine with him: his visits indeed were more properly to the aunt than the nephew; and many of the intelligent ladies in the parish, who, like some very great philosophers, have the happy knack at accounting for every thing, gave out, that there was a particular attachment between them, which wanted only to be matured by some more years of courtship to end in the tenderest connection. In this conclusion indeed, supposing the premises to have been true, they were somewhat justified by the known opinion of the lady who frequently declared herself a friend to the ceremonial of former times, when a lover might have sighed seven years at his mistress's feet, before he was allowed the liberty of kissing her hand. 'Tis true Mrs. Margery was now about her grand climacteric,* no matter: that is just the age when we expect to grow younger. But I verily believe there was nothing in the report; the curate's connection was only that of a genealogist; for in that character he was no way inferior to Mrs. Margery herself. He dealt also in the present times; for he was a politician and a newsmonger.

He had hardly said grace after dinner, when he told Mrs. Margery, that she might soon expect a pair of white gloves, as Sir Harry Benson, he was very well informed, was just going to be married to Miss Walton. Harley spilt the wine he was carrying to his mouth: he had time however to recollect himself before the curate had finished the different particulars of his intelligence, and summing up all the heroism he was master of, filled a bumper and drank to Miss Walton. 'With all my heart,' said the curate, 'the bride that is to be.' Harley would have said bride too; but the word Bride stuck in his throat. His confusion indeed was manifest: but the curate began to enter on some point of descent with Mrs. Margery, and Harley had very soon after an opportunity of leaving them, while they were deeply engaged in a question, whether the name of some great man in the time of Henry the Seventh was Richard or Humphrey.

He did not see his aunt again till supper; the time between he spent in walking, like some troubled ghost, round the place where his treasure lay. He went as far as a little gate, that led into a copse near Mr. Walton's house, to which that gentleman had been so obliging as to let him have a key. He had just begun to open it, when he saw, on a terrass below, Miss Walton walking with a gentleman in a riding-dress, whom he immediately guessed to be Sir Harry Benson. He stopped of a sudden; his hand shook so

much that he could hardly turn the key; he opened the gate
however, and advanced a few paces. The lady's lap-dog pricked
up its ears, and barked: he stopped again.——

> ——'The little dogs and all
> Tray, Blanch, and Sweetheart, see they bark at me!'*

His resolution failed; he slunk back, and locking the gate as softly
as he could, stood on tiptoe looking over the wall till they were
gone. At that instant a shepherd blew his horn: the romantic
melancholy of the sound quite overcame him!—it was the very
note that wanted to be touched—he sighed! he dropped a tear!—
and returned.

  At supper his aunt observed that he was graver than usual; but
she did not suspect the cause: indeed it may seem odd that she
was the only person in the family who had no suspicion of his
attachment to Miss Walton. It was frequently matter of discourse
amongst the servants: perhaps her maiden coldness—but for
those things we need not account.

  In a day or two he was so much master of himself as to be able
to rhime upon the subject. The following pastoral he left, some
time after, on the handle of a tea-kettle, at a neighbouring house
where we were visiting; and as I filled the tea-pot after him, I
happened to put it in my pocket by a similar act of forgetfulness.
It is such as might be expected from a man who makes verses for
amusement. I am pleased with somewhat of good-nature that
runs through it, because I have commonly observed the writers of
those complaints to bestow epithets on their lost mistresses rather
too harsh for the mere liberty of choice, which led them to prefer
another to the poet himself: I do not doubt the vehemence of
their passion; but alas! the sensations of love are something more
than the returns of gratitude.

LAVINIA. A PASTORAL

WHY steals from my bosom the sigh?
  Why fix'd is my gaze on the ground?
Come, give me my pipe, and I'll try
  To banish my cares with the sound.

(sweet melancholy)

Erewhile were its notes of accord
    With the smile of the flow'r-footed muse;
Ah! why by its master implor'd
    Shou'd it now the gay carrol refuse?

'Twas taught by LAVINIA's sweet smile
    In the mirth-loving chorus to join:
Ah me! how unweeting the while!
    LAVINIA——can never be mine!

Another, more happy, the maid
    By fortune is destin'd to bless——
Tho' the hope has forsook that betray'd,
    Yet why shou'd I love her the less?

Her beauties are bright as the morn,
    With rapture I counted them o'er;
Such virtues those beauties adorn,
    I knew her, and prais'd them no more.

I term'd her no goddess of love,
    I call'd not her beauty divine:
These far other passions may prove,   — "The
    But they could not be figures of mine.   living

It ne'er was apparell'd with art,   — lyre"
    On words it could never rely;
It reign'd in the throb of my heart,
    It gleam'd in the glance of my eye.

Oh fool! in the circle to shine
    That fashion's gay daughters approve,
You must speak as the fashions incline;—
    Alas! are there fashions in love?

Yet sure they are simple who prize
    The tongue that is smooth to deceive;
Yet sure she had sense to despise
    The tinsel that folly may weave.

When I talk'd, I have seen her recline
    With an aspect so pensively sweet,——
Tho' I spoke what the shepherds opine,
    A fop were asham'd to repeat.

She is soft as the dew-drops that fall
    From the lip of the sweet-scented pea;
Perhaps, when she smil'd upon all,
    I have thought that she smil'd upon me.

But why of her charms should I tell?
    Ah me! whom her charms have undone!
Yet I love the reflection too well,
    The painful reflection to shun.

Ye souls of more delicate kind,
    Who feast not on pleasure alone,
Who wear the soft sense of the mind,
    To the sons of the world still unknown;

Ye know, tho' I cannot express,
    Why I foolishly doat on my pain;
Nor will ye believe it the less
    That I have not the skill to complain.

I lean on my hand with a sigh,
    My friends the soft sadness condemn;
Yet, methinks, tho' I cannot tell why,
    I should hate to be merry like them.

When I walk'd in the pride of the dawn,
    Methought all the region look'd bright:
Has sweetness forsaken the lawn?
    For, methinks, I grow sad at the sight.

When I stood by the stream, I have thought
    There was mirth in the gurgling soft sound;
But now 'tis a sorrowful note,
    And the banks are all gloomy around!

I have laugh'd at the jest of a friend;
    Now they laugh and I know not the cause,
Tho' I seem with my looks to attend,
    How silly! I ask what it was!

They sing the sweet song of the May,
    They sing it with mirth and with glee;
Sure I once thought the sonnet was gay,
    But now 'tis all sadness to me.

Oh! give me the dubious light
    That gleams thro' the quivering shade;
Oh! give me the horrors of night
    By gloom and by silence array'd!

Let me walk where the soft-rising wave
    Has pictur'd the moon on its breast:
Let me walk where the new-cover'd grave
    Allows the pale lover to rest!

When shall I in its peaceable womb
    Be laid with my sorrows asleep!
Should LAVINIA but chance on my tomb—
    I could die if I thought she would weep.

Perhaps, if the souls of the just
    Revisit these mansions of care,
It may be my favourite trust
    To watch o'er the fate of the fair.

Perhaps the soft thought of her breast
    With rapture more favour'd to warm;
Perhaps, if with sorrow oppress'd,
    Her sorrow with patience to arm.

Then! then! in the tenderest part
    May I whisper, 'Poor COLIN was true;'
And mark if a heave of her heart
    The thought of her COLIN pursue.

THE PUPIL. A FRAGMENT

A matter of education?

* * * * 'BUT as to the higher part of education,* Mr. Harley, the culture of the Mind;—let the feelings be awakened, let the heart be brought forth to its object, placed in the light in which nature would have it stand, and its decisions will ever be just. The world

    Will smile, and smile, and be a villain;*

and the youth, who does not suspect its deceit, will be content to smile with it.—Men will put on the most forbidding aspect in nature, and tell him of the beauty of virtue.

'I have not, under these grey hairs, forgotten that I was once a young man, warm in the pursuit of pleasure, but meaning to be honest as well as happy. I had ideas of virtue, of honour, of benevolence, which I had never been at the pains to define; but I felt my bosom heave at the thoughts of them, and I made the most delightful soliloquies——It is impossible, said I, that there can be half so many rogues as are imagined.

'I travelled, because it is the fashion for young men of my fortune to travel: I had a travelling tutor, which is the fashion too; but my tutor was a gentleman, which it is not always the fashion for tutors to be. His gentility indeed was all he had from his father, whose prodigality had not left him a shilling to support it.

' "I have a favour to ask of you, my dear Mountford," said my father, "which I will not be refused: You have travelled as became a man; neither France nor Italy have made any thing of Mountford, which Mountford before he left England would have been ashamed of: my son Edward goes abroad, would you take him under your protection?"—He blushed—my father's face was scarlet—he pressed his hand to his bosom, as if he had said,—my heart does not mean to offend you. Mountford sighed twice—"I am a proud fool," said he, "and you will pardon it;—there!" (he sighed again) "I can hear of dependence, since it is dependence on my Sedley"—"Dependance!" answered my father; "there can be no such word between us: what is there in 9000 l. a-year that should make me unworthy of Mountford's friendship?"——They embraced; and soon after I set out on my travels, with Mountford for my guardian.

'We were at Milan, where my father happened to have an Italian friend, to whom he had been of some service in England. The count, for he was of quality, was solicitous to return the obligation, by a particular attention to his son: We lived in his palace, visited with his family, were caressed by his friends, and I began to be so well pleased with my entertainment, that I thought of England as of some foreign country.

'The count had a son not much older than myself. At that age a friend is an easy acquisition: we were friends the first night of our acquaintance.

'He introduced me into the company of a set of young gentlemen, whose fortunes gave them the command of pleasure, and whose inclinations incited them to the purchase. After having spent some joyous evenings in their society, it became a sort of habit which I could not miss without uneasiness; and our meetings, which before were frequent, were now stated and regular.

'Sometimes, in the pauses of our mirth, gaming was introduced as an amusement: it was an art in which I was a novice; I received instruction, as other novices, do, by losing pretty largely to my teachers. Nor was this the only evil which Mountford foresaw would arise from the connection I had formed; but a lecture of four injunctions was not his method of reclaiming. He sometimes asked me questions about the company; but they were such as the curiosity of any indifferent man might have prompted: I told him of their wit, their eloquence, their warmth of friendship, and their sensibility of heart; "And their honour," said I, laying my hand on my breast, "is unquestionable." Mountford seemed to rejoice at my good fortune, and begged that I would introduce him to their acquaintance. At the next meeting I introduced him accordingly.

'The conversation was as animated as usual; they displayed all that sprightliness and good-humour which my praises had led Mountford to expect; subjects too of sentiment occurred, and their speeches, particularly those of our friend the son of count Respino, glowed with the warmth of honour, and softened into the tenderness of feeling. Mountford was charmed with his companions; when we parted he made the highest eulogiums upon them: "When shall we see them again?" said he. I was delighted with the demand, and promised to reconduct him on the morrow.

'In going to their place of rendezvous, he took me a little out of the road, to see, as he told me, the performances of a young statuary. When we were near the house in which Mountford said he lived, a boy of about seven years old crossed us in the street. At sight of Mountford he stopped, and grasping his hand, "My dearest Sir," said he, "my father is likely to do well; he will live to pray for you, and to bless you: yes, he will bless you, though you are an Englishman, and some other hard word that the monk talked of this morning which I have forgot, but it meant that you should not go to heaven; but he shall go to heaven, said I, for he has saved my father: come and see him, Sir, that we may be happy."—"My dear, I am engaged at present with this gentleman."—"But he shall come along with you; he is an Englishman too, I fancy; he shall come and learn how an Englishman may go to heaven."—Mountford smiled, and we followed the boy together.

'After crossing the next street, we arrived at the gate of a prison. I seemed surprised at the sight; our little conductor observed it. "Are you afraid, Sir?" said he; "I was afraid once too, but my father and mother are here, and I am never afraid when I am with them." He took my hand, and led me through a dark passage that fronted the gate. When we came to a little door at the end, he tapped; a boy, still younger than himself, opened it to receive us. Mountford entered with a look in which was pictured the benign assurance of a superior being. I followed in silence and amazement.

'On something like a bed lay a man, with a face seemingly emaciated with sickness, and a look of patient dejection; a bundle of dirty shreds served him for a pillow; but he had a better support—the arm of a female who kneeled beside him, beautiful as an angel, but with a fading languor in her countenance, the still life of melancholy, that seemed to borrow its shade from the object on which she gazed. There was a tear in her eye! the sick man kissed it off in its bud, smiling through the dimness of his own!—when she saw Mountford, she crawled forward on the ground and clasped his knees; he raised her from the floor; she threw her arms round his neck, and sobbed out a speech of thankfulness, eloquent beyond the power of language.

'"Compose yourself, my love," said the man on the bed; "but he, whose goodness has caused that emotion, will pardon its effects."—"How is this, Mountford?" said I; "what do I see? what must I do?"——"You see," replied the stranger, "a wretch, sunk in poverty, starving in prison, stretched on a sick bed! but that is little:——there are his wife and children, wanting the bread which he has not to give them! Yet you cannot easily imagine the conscious serenity of his mind; in the gripe of affliction, his heart swells with the pride of virtue! it can even look down with pity on the man whose cruelty has wrung it almost to bursting. You are, I fancy, a friend of Mr. Mountford's; come nearer and I will tell you; for, short as my story is, I can hardly command breath enough for a recital. The son of count Respino" (I started as if I had trod on a viper) "has long had a criminal passion for my wife: this her prudence had concealed from me; but he had lately the boldness to declare it to myself. He promised me affluence in exchange for honour; and threatened misery, as its attendant, if I kept it. I treated him with the contempt he deserved: the consequence was, that he hired a couple of bravoes (for I am persuaded they acted under his direction) who attempted to assassinate me in the street; but I made such a defence as obliged them to fly, after having given me two or three stabs, none of which however were mortal. But his revenge was not thus to be disappointed: in the little dealings of my trade I had contracted some debts, of which he had made himself master for my ruin; I was confined here at his suit, when not yet recovered from the wounds I had received; that dear woman, and these two boys, followed me, that we might starve together; but Providence interposed, and sent Mr. Mountford to our support: he has relieved my family from the gnawings of hunger, and rescued me from death, to which a fever, consequent on my wounds, and increased by the want of every necessary, had almost reduced me."

'"Inhuman villain!" I exclaimed, lifting up my eyes to heaven. "Inhuman indeed!" said the lovely woman who stood at my side: "Alas! Sir, what had we done to offend him? what had these little ones done, that they should perish in the toils of his vengeance?"——I reached a pen which stood in an ink-standish at the bed-side—"May I ask what is the amount of the sum for which you are imprisoned?"—"I was able," he replied, "to pay all but 500 crowns."—I wrote a draught on the banker with whom I had a credit from my father for 2500, and presenting it to the stranger's wife, "You will receive, Madam, on presenting this note, a sum more than sufficient for your husband's discharge; the remainder I leave for his industry to improve." I would have left the room: each of them laid hold of one of my hands; the children clung to my coat:—Oh! Mr. Harley, methinks I feel their gentle violence at this moment; it beats here with delight inexpressible!—"Stay, Sir," said he, "I do not mean attempting to thank you;" (he took a pocket-book from under his pillow) "let me but know what name I shall place here next to Mr. Mountford's?"—Sedley——he writ it down—"An Englishman too I presume."—"He shall go to heaven notwithstanding," said the boy who had been our guide. It began to be too much for me; I squeezed his hand that was clasped in mine; his wife's I pressed to my lips, and burst from the place to give vent to the feelings that laboured within me.

'"Oh! Mountford!" said I, when he had overtaken me at the door: "It is time," replied he, "that we should think of our appointment; young Respino and his friends are waiting us."—— "Damn him, damn him!" said I; "let us leave Milan instantly; but soft——I will be calm; Mountford, your pencil." I wrote on a slip of paper,

'To Signor RESPINO,

'"When you receive this I am at a distance from Milan. Accept of my thanks for the civilities I have received from you and your family. As to the friendship with which you were pleased to honour me, the prison, which I have just left, has exhibited a scene to cancel it for ever. You may possibly be merry with your companions at my weakness, as I suppose you will term it. I give you leave for derision: you may affect a triumph; I shall feel it.

EDWARD SEDLEY."

'"You may send this if you will," said Mountford coolly; "but still Respino is *a man of honour*; the world will continue to call him so."—"It is probable," I answered, "they may; I envy not the appellation. If this is the world's honour, if these men are the guides of its manners"—"Tut!" said Mountford, "do you eat macaroni?*"——'

* * * * *

[At this place had the greatest depredations of the curate begun. There were so very few connected passages of the subsequent chapters remaining, that even the partiality of an editor could not offer them to the public. I discovered, from some scattered sentences, that they were of much the same tenor with the preceding; recitals of little adventures, in which the dispositions of a man, sensible to judge, and still more warm to feel, had room to unfold themselves. Some instruction, and some example, I make no doubt they contained; but it is likely that many of those, whom chance has led to a perusal of what I have already presented, may have read it with little pleasure, and will feel no disappointment from the want of those parts which I have been unable to procure: to such as may have expected the intricacies of a novel, a few incidents in a life undistinguished, except by some features of the heart, cannot have afforded much entertainment.

Harley's own story, from the mutilated passages I have mentioned, as well as from some inquiries I was at the trouble of making in the country, I found to have been simple to excess. His mistress I could perceive was not married to Sir Harry Benson: but it would seem, by one of the following chapters, which is still entire, that Harley had not profited on the occasion by making any declaration of his own passion, after those of the other had been unsuccessful. The state of his health for some part of this period, appears to have been such as to forbid any thoughts of that kind: he had been seized with a very dangerous fever, caught by attending old Edwards in one of an infectious kind. From this he had recovered but imperfectly, and though he had no formed complaint, his health was manifestly on the decline.

It appears that the sagacity of some friend had at length pointed out to his aunt a cause from which this might be supposed to proceed, to wit, his hopeless love for Miss Walton; for according to the conceptions of the world, the love of a man of

Harley's fortune for the heiress of 4000 l. a-year, is indeed desperate. Whether it was so in this case may be gathered from the next chapter, which, with the two subsequent, concluding the performance, have escaped those accidents that proved fatal to the rest.]

CHAPTER LV

HE SEES MISS WALTON, AND IS HAPPY

HARLEY was one of those few friends whom the malevolence of fortune had yet left me: I could not therefore but be sensibly concerned for his present indisposition; there seldom passed a day on which I did not make inquiry about him.

The physician who attended him had informed me the evening before, that he thought him considerably better than he had been for some time past. I called next morning to be confirmed in a piece of intelligence so welcome to me.

When I entered his apartment, I found him sitting on a couch, leaning on his hand, with his eye turned upwards in the attitude of thoughtful inspiration. His look had always an open benignity, which commanded esteem; there was now something more—a gentle triumph in it.

He rose, and met me with his usual kindness. When I gave him the good accounts I had had from his physician, 'I am foolish enough,' said he, 'to rely but little, in this instance, upon physic: my presentiment may be false; but I think I feel myself approaching to my end, by steps so easy, that they woo me to approach it.

'There is a certain dignity in retiring from life at a time, when the infirmities of age have not sapped our faculties. This world, my dear Charles, was a scene in which I never much delighted. I was not formed for the bustle of the busy, nor the dissipation of the gay: a thousand things occurred where I blushed for the impropriety of my conduct when I thought on the world, though my reason told me I should have blushed to have done otherwise.—It was a scene of dissimulation, of restraint, of disappointment. I leave it to enter on that state, which, I have learned to believe, is replete with the genuine happiness attendant upon virtue. I look back on the tenor of my life, with the consciousness of few great offences to account for. There are blemishes, I confess, which deform in some degree the picture. But I know the benignity of the Supreme Being, and rejoice at the thoughts of its exertion in my favour. My mind expands at the thought I shall enter into the society of the blessed, wise as angels, with the simplicity of children.' He had by this time clasped my hand, and found it wet by a tear which had just fallen upon it.— His eye began to moisten too—we sat for some time silent—At last, with an attempt to a look of more composure, 'There are some remembrances' (said Harley) 'which rise involuntarily on my heart, and make me almost wish to live. I have been blessed with a few friends, who redeem my opinion of mankind. I recollect, with the tenderest emotion, the scenes of pleasure I have passed among them; but we shall meet again, my friend, never to be separated. There are some feelings which perhaps are too tender to be suffered by the world. The world is in general selfish, interested, and unthinking, and throws the imputation of romance or melancholy on every temper more susceptible than its own. I cannot think but in those regions which I contemplate, if there is any thing of mortality left about us, that these feelings will subsist;—they are called,—perhaps they are—weaknesses here;—but there may be some better modifications of them in heaven, which may deserve the name of virtues.' He sighed as he spoke these last words. He had scarcely finished them, when the door opened, and his aunt appeared leading in Miss Walton. 'My dear,' says she, 'here is Miss Walton, who has been so kind as to come and inquire for you herself.' I could observe a transient glow upon his face. He rose from his seat—'If to know Miss Walton's goodness,' said he, 'be a title to deserve it, I have some claim.' She begged him to resume his seat, and placed herself on the sofa beside him. I took my leave. Mrs. Margery accompanied me to the door. He was left with Miss Walton alone. She inquired anxiously about his health. 'I believe,' said he, 'from the accounts which my physicians unwillingly give me, that they have no great hopes of my recovery.'—She started as he spoke; but recollecting herself immediately, endeavoured to flatter him into a belief that his apprehensions were groundless. 'I know,' said he, 'that it is usual with persons at my time of life to have these hopes which your kindness suggests; but I would not wish to be deceived. To meet death as becomes a man, is a privilege bestowed on few.—I would endeavour to make it mine;—nor do I think that I can ever be better prepared for it than now:—It is that chiefly which determines the fitness of its approach.'—'Those sentiments,' answered Miss Walton, 'are just: but your good sense, Mr. Harley, will own, that life has its proper value.—As the province of virtue, life is ennobled; as such, it is to be desired.—To virtue has the Supreme Director of all things assigned rewards enough even here to fix its attachment.'

The subject began to overpower her.—Harley lifted his eyes from the ground—'There are,' said he, 'in a very low voice, there are attachments, Miss Walton'—His glance met hers—They both betrayed a confusion, and were both instantly withdrawn.— He paused some moments—'I am in such a state as calls for sincerity, let that also excuse it—It is perhaps the last time we shall ever meet. I feel something particularly solemn in the acknowledgement, yet my heart swells to make it, awed as it is by a sense of my presumption, by a sense of your perfections'—He paused again—'Let it not offend you to know their power over one so unworthy—It will, I believe, soon cease to beat, even with that feeling which it shall lose the latest.—To love Miss Walton could not be a crime;—if to declare it is one—the expiation will be made.'—Her tears were now flowing without controul.—'Let me intreat you,' said she, 'to have better hopes—Let not life be so indifferent to you; if my wishes can put any value on it—I will not pretend to misunderstand you—I know your worth—I have known it long—I have esteemed it—What would you have me say?—I have loved it as it deserved.'——He seized her hand—a languid colour reddened his cheek—a smile brightened faintly in his eye. As he gazed on her, it grew dim, it fixed, it closed—He sighed, and fell back on his seat.—Miss Walton screamed at the sight—His aunt and the servants rushed into the room—They found them lying motionless together.—His physician happened to call at that instant.—Every art was tried to recover them—With Miss Walton they succeeded—But Harley was gone for ever!

CHAPTER LVI

THE EMOTIONS OF THE HEART

I ENTERED the room where his body lay; I approached it with reverence, not fear: I looked; the recollection of the past crowded upon me. I saw that form, which, but a little before, was animated with a soul which did honour to humanity, stretched without sense or feeling before me. 'Tis a connection we cannot easily forget:—I took his hand in mine; I repeated his name involuntarily:—I felt a pulse in every vein at the sound. I looked earnestly in his face; his eye was closed, his lip pale and motionless. There is an enthusiasm in sorrow that forgets impossibility; I wondered that it was so. The sight drew a prayer from my heart; it was the voice of frailty and of man! the confusion of my mind began to subside into thought; I had time to weep!

I turned, with the last farewel upon my lips, when I observed old Edwards standing behind me. I looked him full in the face; but his eye was fixed on another object: he pressed between me and the bed, and stood gazing on the breathless remains of his benefactor. I spoke to him I know not what; but he took no notice of what I said, and remained in the same attitude as before. He stood some minutes in that posture, then turned and walked towards the door. He paused as he went;—he returned a second time: I could observe his lips move as he looked; but the voice they would have uttered was lost. He attempted going again; and a third time he returned as before.—I saw him wipe his cheek; then covering his face with his hands, his breast heaving with the most convulsive throbs, he flung out of the room.

THE CONCLUSION

HE had hinted that he should like to be buried in a certain spot near the grave of his mother. This is a weakness; but it is universally incident to humanity: 'tis at least a memorial for those who survive; for some indeed a slender memorial will serve; and the soft affections, when they are busy that way, will build their structures, were it but on the paring of a nail.

He was buried in the place he had desired. It was shaded by an old tree, the only one in the church-yard, in which was a cavity worn by time. I have sat with him in it, and counted the tombs. The last time we passed there, methought he looked wistfully on that tree: there was a branch of it, that bent towards us, waving in the wind; he waved his hand, as if he mimicked its motion. There was something predictive in his look! perhaps it is foolish to remark it; but there are times and places when I am a child at those things.

I sometimes visit his grave; I sit in the hollow of the tree. It is worth a thousand homilies! every nobler feeling rises within me! every beat of my heart awakens a virtue!—but it will make you hate the world—No: there is such an air of gentleness around, that I can hate nothing; but, as to the world—I pity the men of it.

FINIS

APPENDIX 1

HENRY MACKENZIE, *THE LOUNGER*, NO. 20
(SATURDAY, 18 JUNE 1785)

The Lounger and *The Mirror*, both of which Mackenzie edited, aimed to replicate in Edinburgh the circulation of anecdote and conversation among the polite that Addison and Steele had established in their periodicals *The Guardian* and *The Spectator* earlier in the century in London. (That Scott called Mackenzie 'Our Scottish Addison' in dedicating *Waverley* to him testifies to the success of this endeavour.) Both periodicals mixed fiction with discursive essays such as the following, on the novel.

For Mackenzie the novel is the form 'beyond any other, open to the judgement of the people' but appeals mainly to 'the young and the indolent'—and indeed was 'frequently put into the hands of youth for imitation as well as amusement'. The influence of fiction may be in preaching a vicious 'refinement', yet Mackenzie suggests that what counts as vice has changed relative to the increased cultivation of the era—a suggestion of historical relativism in line with the Scottish Enlightenment agenda alluded to in the Introduction. Only then does he attack sentimental fiction specifically, not just its excess and 'overstrained delicacy', but its tendency to question civic duties in favour of 'the exertions of generosity, of benevolence, and of compassion'. He does not, however, attack sentiment *tout court* but, as again in *The Man of Feeling*, 'that sickly sort of sentiment' which is associated with the French, and the 'degradation' of the sentimental novel. Perhaps he has Rousseau in mind here, just as later, in alluding to 'that character of mingled virtue and vice', he is thinking of Richardson—both are favourites of the narrator of *The Man of Feeling* in the original edition. (Significantly, the name of Rousseau is omitted from the second edition, the copy text for this edition—see Note on the Text.) The tradition of a writer of fiction attacking the vicious tendency of fiction, sometimes from within a work of fiction itself, is as old as the western novel tradition. In *The Man of Feeling* Emily Atkins is ruined by the influence of novel-reading (p. 43). So the paradox of Mackenzie, fourteen years on, attacking that which had established his own reputation is more apparent than actual. The 'separation of conscience from feeling' he deprecates here is what *The Man of Feeling* was already debating.

We imitate the vices of the great, mistaking them for

Decipit exemplar vitiis imitabile*.—HOR.

the causes of their greatness

NO species of composition is more generally read by one class of readers, or more undervalued by another, than that of the novel. Its favourable reception from the young and the indolent, to whom the exercise of imagination is delightful, and the labour of thought is irksome, needs not be wondered at; but the contempt which it meets from the more respectable class of literary men, it may perhaps be entitled to plead that it does not deserve. Considered in the abstract, as containing an interesting relation of events, illustrative of the manners and characters of mankind, it surely merits a higher station in the world of letters than is generally assigned it. If it has not the dignity, it has at least most of the difficulties, of the epic or the drama. The conduct of its fable, the support of its characters, the contrivance of its incidents, and its development of the passions, require a degree of invention, judgment, taste, and feeling, not much, if at all, inferior to those higher departments of writing, for the composition of which a very uncommon portion of genius is supposed to be requisite. Those difficulties are at the same time heightened by the circumstance, of this species of writing being, beyond any other, open to the judgment of the people; because it represents domestic scenes and situations in private life, in the execution of which any man may detect errors and discover blemishes, while the author has neither the pomp of poetry, nor the decoration of the stage, to cover or to conceal them.

To this circumstance, however, may perhaps be imputed the degradation into which it has fallen. As few endowments were necessary to judge, so few have been supposed necessary to compose a novel; and all whose necessities or vanity prompted them to write, betook themselves to a field, which, as they imagined, it required no extent of information or depth of learning to cultivate, but in which a heated imagination, or an excursive fancy, were alone sufficient to succeed; and men of genius and of knowledge, despising a province in which such competitors were to be met, retired from it in disgust, and left it in the hands of the unworthy.

The effects of this have been felt, not only in the debasement of the novel in point of literary merit, but in another particular still more material, in its perversion from a moral or instructive purpose to one directly the reverse. Ignorance and dulness are seldom long inoffensive, but generally support their own native insignificance by an alliance with voluptuousness and vice.

Even of those few novels which superior men have written, it cannot always be said, that they are equally calculated to improve as to delight. Nor is this only to be objected to some who have been professedly less scrupulous in that particular; but I am afraid may be also imputed to those whose works were meant to convey no bad impression, but, on the contrary, were intended to aid the cause of virtue, and to hold out patterns of the most exalted benevolence.

I am not, however, disposed to carry the idea of the dangerous tendency of all novels quite so far as some rigid moralists have done. As promoting a certain refinement of mind, they operate like all other works of genius and feeling, and have indeed a more immediate tendency to produce it than most others, from their treating of those very subjects which the reader will find around him in the world, and their containing those very situations in which he himself may not improbably at some time or other be placed. Those who object to them as inculcating precepts, and holding forth examples, of a refinement which virtue does not require, and which honesty is better without, do not perhaps sufficiently attend to the period of society which produces them. The code of morality must necessarily be enlarged in proportion to that state of manners to which cultivated æras give birth. As the idea of property made a crime of theft, as the invention of oaths made falsehood perjury; so the necessary refinement in manners of highly-polished nations creates a variety of duties and of offences, which men in ruder, and, it may be (for I enter not into that question,) happier periods of society, could never have imagined.

The principal danger of novels, as forming a mistaken and pernicious system of morality, seems to me to arise from that contrast between one virtue or excellence and another, that war of duties which is to be found in many of them, particularly in that species called the sentimental. These have been chiefly borrowed from our neighbours the French, whose style of manners, and the very powers of whose language, give them a great advantage in the delineation of that nicety, that subtilty of feeling, those entanglements of delicacy, which are so much interwoven with the characters and conduct of the chief personages in many of their most celebrated novels. In this rivalship of virtues and of duties, those are always likely to be preferred which in truth and reason are subordinate, and those to be degraded which ought to be paramount. The last, being of that great cardinal sort which must be common, because they apply to the great leading relations and circumstances of life, have an appearance less dignified and heroic than the others, which, as they come forth only on extraordinary occasions, are more apt to attract the view and excite the admiration of beholders. The duty to parents is contrasted with the ties of friendship and of love; the virtues of justice, of prudence, of economy, are put in competition with the exertions of generosity, of benevolence, and of compassion: and even of these virtues of sentiment there are still more refined divisions, in which the overstrained delicacy of the persons represented always leads them to act from the motive least obvious, and therefore generally the least reasonable.

In the enthusiasm of sentiment there is much the same danger as in the enthusiasm of religion, of substituting certain impulses and feelings of what may be called a visionary kind, in the place of real practical duties, which in morals, as in theology, we might not improperly denominate good works. In morals, as in religion, there are not wanting instances of refined sentimentalists, who are contented with talking of virtues which they never practise, who pay in words what they owe in actions; or, perhaps, what is fully as dangerous, who open their minds to impressions which never have any effect upon their conduct, but are considered as something foreign to and distinct from it. This separation of conscience from feeling is a depravity of the most pernicious sort; it eludes the strongest obligation to rectitude, it blunts the strongest incitement to virtue; when the ties of the first bind the sentiment and not the will, and the rewards of the latter crown not the heart but the imagination.

That creation of refined and subtile feeling, reared by the authors of the works to which I allude, has an ill effect, not only on our ideas of virtue, but also on our estimate of happiness. That sickly sort of refinement creates imaginary evils and distresses, and imaginary blessings and enjoyments, which embitter the common disappointments, and depreciate the common attainments of life. This affects the temper doubly, both with respect to ourselves and others; with respect to ourselves, from what we think ought to be our lot; with regard to others, from what we think ought to be their sentiments. It inspires a certain childish pride of our own superior delicacy, and an unfortunate contempt of the plain worth, the ordinary but useful occupations and ideas of those around us.

The reproach which has been sometimes made to novels, of exhibiting 'such faultless monsters as the world ne'er saw,' may be just on the score of entertainment to their readers, to whom the delineation of uniform virtue, except when it is called into striking situations, will no doubt be insipid. But, in point of moral tendency, the opposite character is much more reprehensible; I mean that character of mingled virtue and vice which is to be found in some of the best of our novels. Instances will readily occur to every reader, where the hero of the performance has violated, in one page, the most sacred laws of society, to whom, by the mere turning of the leaf, we are to be reconciled, whom we are to be made to love and admire, for the beauty of some humane, or the brilliancy of some heroic action. It is dangerous thus to bring us into the society of vice, though introduced or accompanied by virtue. In the application to ourselves, in which the moral tendency of all imaginary characters must be supposed to consist, this nourishes and supports a very common kind of self-deception, by which men are apt to balance their faults by the consideration of their good qualities; an account which, besides the fallacy of its principle, can scarcely fail to be erroneous, from our natural propensity to state our faults at their lowest, and our good qualities at their highest rate.

I have purposely pointed my observations, not to that common herd of novels (the wretched offspring of circulating libraries) which are despised for their insignificance, or proscribed for their immorality; but to the errors, as they appear to me, of those admired ones which are frequently put into the hands of youth for imitation as well as amusement. Of youth it is essential to preserve the imagination sound as well as pure, and not to allow them to forget, amidst the intricacies of sentiment, or the dreams of sensibility, the truths of reason, or the laws of principle.

APPENDIX 2

FROM HENRY MACKENZIE, *JULIA DE ROUBIGNÉ*
LETTER XXVIII: *SAVILLON TO BEAUVARIS*

Like *The Man of Feeling*, Mackenzie's third novel, *Julia de Roubigné*, is introduced as 'a bundle of papers' saved from an ignomini-
ous fate as scrap paper, on this occasion destined for a grocery shop.
Again, a tale of sentimental suffering is told in an apparently ran-
dom order, and again the disruption of conventional narrative suggests that, in the words of the 'editor', 'it is not so much on story, as
sentiment, that their interest with the Reader must depend'. As in
The Man of Feeling, the fragmentariness of the text allows for the
introduction of disparate material, including the reformist episode
we reproduce here. Setting out in search of a fortune, Julia's
admirer, Savillon, has travelled to Martinique to work on his uncle's
slave plantation: the tone of the episode is undoubtedly humanitar-
ian, but as in the Indian chapter in *The Man of Feeling*, it is also
ultimately a small-scale, local episode rather than a sustained
polemic.

The text here is reproduced from *The Works of Henry Mackenzie,
Esq.*, 8 vols. (Edinburgh, 1808), vol. 3.

A THOUSAND thanks for your last letter. When you know how much I
enjoyed the unwieldy appearance of the packet, with my friend's hand
on the back of it, you will not grudge the time it cost you. It is just
such as I wished: your scene-painting is delightful. No man is more
susceptible of local attachments than I; and, with the Atlantic
between, there is not a stone in France which I can remember with
indifference.

Yet I am happier here than I could venture to expect. Had I been
left to my own choice, I should probably have sat down in solitude, to
think of the past, and enjoy my reflections; but I have been forced to
do better. There is an active duty which rewards every man in the
performance; and my uncle has so contrived matters, that I have had
very little time unemployed. He has been liberal of instruction, and, I
hope, has found me willing to be instructed. Our business, indeed, is
not very intricate; but, in the simplest occupations, there are a

thousand little circumstances which experience alone can teach us. In certain departments, however, I have tried projects of my own: Some of them have failed in the end, but all gave me pleasure in the pursuit. In one I have been successful beyond expectation; and in that one I was the most deeply interested, because it touched the cause of humanity.

To a man not callous from habit, the treatment of the negroes, in the plantations here, is shocking. I felt it strongly, and could not forbear expressing my sentiments to my uncle. He allowed them to be natural, but pleaded necessity, in justification of those severites, which his overseers sometimes used towards his laves. I ventured to doubt this proposition, and begged he would suffer me to try a different mode of government in one plantation, the produce of which he had already allotted to my management. He consented, though with the belief that I should succeed very ill in the experiment.

I began by endeavouring to ingratiate myself with such of the slaves as could best speak the language of my country; but I found this was a manner they did not understand, and that, from a white, the appearance of indulgence carried the suspicion of treachery. Most of them, to whom rigour had become habitual, took the advantage of its remitting, to neglect their work altogether; but this only served to convince me, that my plan was a good one, and that I should undoubtedly profit, if I could establish some other motive, whose impulse was more steady than those of punishment and terror.

By continuing the mildness of my conduct, I at last obtained a degree of willingness in the service of some; and I was still induced to believe, that the most savage and sullen among them had principles of gratitude, which a good master might improve to his advantage.

One slave, in particular, had for some time attracted my notice, from that gloomy fortitude with which he bore the hardships of his situation.—Upon enquiring of the overseer, he told me, that this slave, whom he called Yambu, though, from his youth and appearance of strength, he had been accounted valuable, yet, from the untractable stubbornness of his disposition, was worth less money than almost any other in my uncle's possession.—This was a language natural to the overseer. I answered him, in his own style, that I hoped to improve his price some hundreds of livres. On being further informed, that several of his fellow-slaves had come from the same part of the Guinea coast with him, I sent for one of them who could speak tolerable French, and questioned him about Yambu. He told me, that, in their own country, Yambu was master of them all; that they had been taken prisoners, when fighting in his cause, by another prince, who, in one battle, was more fortunate than theirs; that he had sold them to some white men, who came in a great ship to their coast; that they were afterwards brought hither, where other white men purchased them from the first, and set them to work where I saw them; but that when they died, and went beyond the Great Mountains, Yambu should be their master again.

I dismissed the negro, and called this Yambu before me.

When he came, he seemed to regard me with an eye of perfect indifference. One who had enquired no further, would have concluded him possessed of that stupid insensibility, which Europeans often mention as an apology for their cruelties. I took his hand; he considered this a prologue to chastisement, and turned his back to receive the lashes he supposed me ready to inflict. 'I wish to be the friend of Yambu,' said I. He made me no answer: I let go his hand, and he suffered it to drop to its former posture. 'Can this man have been a prince in Africa?' said I to myself.—I reflected for a moment.—'Yet what should he now do, if he has?—Just what I see him do. I have seen a deposed sovereign at Paris; but in Europe, kings are artificial beings, like their subjects.—Silence is the only throne which adversity has left to princes.

'I fear,' said I to him, 'you have been sometimes treated harshly by the overseer; but you shall be treated so no more; I wish all my people to be happy.' He looked on me now for the first time.—'Can you speak my language, or shall I call for some of your friends, who can explain what you would say to me?' 'I speak no say to you,' he replied in his broken French.—'And you will not be my friend?'—'No'—'Even if I should deserve it?'—'You a white man.'—I felt the rebuke as I ought. 'But all white men are not overseers. What shall I do to make you think me a good man?'—'Use men goodly.'—'I mean to do so, and you among the first, Yambu.'—'Be good for Yambu's people; do your please with Yambu.'

Just then the bell rung as a summons for the negroes to go to work: he made a few steps towards the door. 'Would you now go to work,' said I, 'if you were at liberty to avoid it?' 'You make go for whip, and no man love go.' — 'I will go along with you, though I am not obliged; for I chuse to work sometimes rather than be idle.'—'Chuse work, no work at all,' said Yambu.—'Twas the very principle on which my system was founded.

I took him with me into the house when our task was over. 'I wrought chuse work,' said I, 'Yambu, yet I did less than you.'—'Yambu do chuse work then too?'—'You shall do so always,' answered I; 'from this moment you are mine no more!'—'You sell me other white men then?'—'No, you are free, and may do whatever you please!'—'Yambu's please no here, no this country,' he replied, waving his hand, and looking wistfully towards the sea.—'I cannot give you back your country, Yambu; but I can make this one better for you. You can make it better for me too, and for your people!' 'Speak Yambu that,' said he eagerly, 'and be good man!'—'You would not,' said I, 'make your people work by the whip, as you see the overseers do?'—'Oh! no, no whip!'—'Yet they must work, else we shall have no sugars to buy them meat and clothing with.'—(He put his hand to his brow, as if I had started a difficulty he was unable to overcome.)—'Then you shall have the command of them, and they shall work chuse work for Yambu.'—He looked askance, as if he doubted the truth of what I said; I called the negro with whom I had the first conversation about him, and, pointing to Yambu, 'Your master,' said I, 'is now free, and may leave you when he pleases!'—'Yambu no leave you,' said he to the negro warmly.—'But he may accompany Yambu if he chuses.'—Yambu shook his head.—'Master,' said his former subject, 'where we go? leave good white men and go to bad; for much bad white men in this country.'—'Then if you think it better, you shall both stay; Yambu shall be my friend, and help me to raise sugars for the good of us all: you shall have no overseer but Yambu, and shall work no more than he bids you.'—The negro fell at my feet and kissed them; Yambu stood silent, and I saw a tear on his cheek.—'This man has been a prince in Africa!' said I to myself.

I did not mean to deceive them. Next morning I called those negroes, who had formerly been in his service, together, and told them, that, while they continued in the plantation, Yambu was to superintend their work; that if they chose to leave him and me, they were at liberty to go; and that, if found idle or unworthy, they should not be allowed to stay. He has, accordingly, ever since had the command of his former subjects, and superintended their work in a particular quarter of the plantation; and having been declared free, according to the mode prescribed by the laws of the island, has a certain portion of ground allotted him, the produce of which is his property. I have had the satisfaction of observing those men, under the feeling of good treatment, and the idea of liberty, do more than almost double their number subject to the whip of an overseer. I am under no apprehension of desertion or mutiny; they work with the willingness of freedom, yet are mine with more than the obligation of slavery.

I have been often tempted to doubt, whether there is not an error in the whole plan of negro servitude; and whether whites, or creoles born in the West Indies, or perhaps cattle, after the manner of European husbandry, would not do the business better and cheaper than the slaves do? The money which the latter cost at first, the sickness (often owing to despondency of mind) to which they are liable after their arrival, and the proportion that die in consequence of it, make the machine, if it may be so called, of a plantation, extremely expensive in its operations. In the list of slaves belonging to a wealthy planter, it would astonish you to see the number unfit for service, pining under disease, a burden on their master.—I am talking only as a merchant; but as a man—Good heavens! when I think of the many thousands of my fellow-creatures groaning under servitude and misery!—Great God! hast thou peopled those regions of thy world for the purpose of casting out their inhabitants to chains and torture?—No; thou gavest them a land teeming with good things, and lighted'st up thy sun to bring forth spontaneous plenty; but the refinements of man, ever at war with thy works, have changed this scene of profusion and luxuriance into a theatre of rapine, of slavery, and of murder!

Forgive the warmth of this apostrophe! Here it would not be understood; even my uncle, whose heart is far from a hard one, would smile at my romance, and tell me that things must be so. Habit, the tyrant of nature and of reason, is deaf to the voice of either; here she stifles humanity, and debases the species;—for the master of slaves has seldom the soul of a man.

This is not difficult to be accounted for:—from his infancy he is made callous to those feelings which soften at once and ennoble our nature. Children must, of necessity, first exert those towards domestics, because the society of domestics is the first they enjoy; here they are taught to command, for the sake of commanding; to beat and torture, for pure amusement;—their reason and good-nature improve as may be expected.

Among the legends of a European nursery, are stories of captives delivered, of slaves released, who had pined for years in the durance of unmerciful enemies.—Could we suppose its infant audience transported to the sea-shore, where a ship laden with slaves is just landing; the question would be universal, 'Who shall set these poor people free?'—The young West Indian asks his father to buy a boy for him, that he may have something to vent his spite on when he is peevish.

Methinks, too, these people lose a sort of connection, which is of more importance in life than most of the relationships we enjoy. The ancient, the tried domestic of a family, is one of its most useful members; one of its most assured supports. My friend, the ill-fated Roubigné has not one relation who has stood by him in the shipwreck of his fortunes; but the storm could not sever from their master his faithful Le Blanc, or the venerable Lasune.

Oh, Beauvaris! I sometimes sit down alone, and, transporting myself into the little circle at Roubigné's, grow sick of the world, and hate the part which I am obliged to perform in it.

APPENDIX 3

This 'Index to Tears' appeared first in the edition of *The Man of Feeling by Henry Mackenzie*, edited by Professor Henry Morley (Cassell and Company, Ltd., London, Paris, New York and Melbourne, 1886). Page numbers are keyed to the text of our edition.

Morley gives no contextualizing comments on his index: it is as though the repertory of sentimental effects Walter Scott identifies in the novel in his biographical essay on Mackenzie has become a repertory of mirthful effects, perhaps to be read aloud in the Victorian parlour to an audience only needing to hear these categories of tears in order to trigger a rather different physical response. We include it because, as a kind of *index prohibitorum* of excessively sentimental effects, it demonstrates the change in reading habits and tastes in the more than a century since the novel's publication.

INDEX TO TEARS
(*Choking, &c, not counted.*)

'Odds but should have wept'	5
Tear, given, 'cordial drop' repeated	8
" like Cestus of Cytherea	12
" one on a cheek	15
'I will not weep'	15
Tears add energy to benediction	15
" tribute of some	26
" blessings on	26
I would weep too	26
Not an unmoistened eye	27
Do you weep again?	27
Hand bathed with tears	27
Tears, burst into	27
" sobbing and shedding	38
" burst into	38
" virtue in these	38
" he wept at the recollection of her	41
" glister of new-washed	41
Sweet girl (here she wept)	48
I could only weep	48

Tears, saw his   50
"   burst into   50
"   wrung from the heart   51
"   feet bathed with   51
Tears, mingled, *i.e.*, his with hers   51
"   voice lost in   55
Eye met with a tear   55
Tear stood in eye   65
Tears, face bathed with   67
Dropped one tear, no more   67
Tears, press-gang could scarce keep from   69
Big drops wetted gray beard   70
Tears, shower of   71
"   scarce forced—blubbered like a boy   71
Moistened eye   72
Tears choked utterance   73
I have wept many a time   73
Girl wept, brother sobbed   74
Harley kissed off her tears as they flowed, and wept
    between every kiss   74
Tears flowing down cheeks   75
"   gushed afresh   75
Beamy moisture   78
A tear dropped   84
Tear in her eye, the sick man kissed it off in its
    bud, smiling through the dimness of his own   90
Hand wet by tear, just fallen   95
Tears flowing without control   96
Cheek wiped (at the end of the last chapter)   97

EXPLANATORY NOTES

Notes marked (V) are by Brian Vickers.
Notes cited as Petersen are from E. H. Peterson, *A Critical Edition of Henry Mackenzie's* 'Man of Feeling', unpublished D. Phil. thesis, Oxford University (1990).

3 *made a point on a piece of fallow ground*: the dog smells a scent and makes straight for a particular spot across a ploughed but unplanted field.

All is vanity and vexation of spirit: Ecclesiastes 1: 14, 'I have seen all the works that are done under the sun; and, behold, all is vanity and vexation of spirit'; the book is traditionally ascribed to the Israelite king Solomon and maintains a generally pessimistic view of all human activity.

a venerable pile, to which the inclosure belonged: the house in the fields of which the narrator and curate have been shooting.

the only mark of human art ... view of the cascade: the brief gesture towards a fashionably 'natural' landscape garden may suggest Harley's good taste and good nature or the artifice involved in producing the 'natural': both are important in Mackenzie's development of Harley as a man of feeling. See *The Lounger*, nos. 3, 87, 89.

4 *His history!*: the term here implies the popular but scandalous genre of 'secret histories' which claimed to record the more lurid aspects of the lives of public figures; thus, private individuals should not have a 'history'.

te–totum: a game of chance played with a four-sided disc or die.

medley: the narrator continues the musical analogy inherent in the curate's 'strain', but stresses the positive aspects of a narrative without apparent form.

German Illustrissimi: perhaps a reference to the 'enlightened' writings of German secret societies, or more broadly to the 'greats' of German literature. Petersen writes: 'The reference is to the philosophers or logicians who were sniped at for their rigidity of thinking. Pope refers to this rigidity in *The Dunciad*, 4.195–8, 'Each staunch Polemic, stubborn as a rock, | Each Fierce Logician, still expelling Locke, | Came whip and spur, and dash'd thro' thin and thick | On German Crouzaz, and Dutch Burgersdyck' (Petersen).

5 *a Marmontel, or a Richardson*: Jean Francois Marmontel (1723–99), novelist, critic, and dramatist whose *Contes moreaux* (1761) combined morality and sentiment in a series of highly fashionable and much-imitated tales; Samuel Richardson (1689–1761), author of *Pamela* and *Clarissa*, works which set the model for later sentimental fiction.

7 *hic jacet*: Latin for 'here lies' but had come to signify a tombstone or epitaph (Petersen).

8 *bare 250 l. a year*: £250 per annum would place them on the very edge of polite gentility and allow for few luxuries.

10 *Coke upon Lyttelton*: Sir Edward Coke (1552–1634) published an explanation and defence of the Common Law in his *Institutes* (1624–44), the first part of which was a commentary on an account of property law by Sir Thomas Littleton (1422–81).

11 *cholic-water*: medicine for abdominal pain.

crown-lands: lands owned by the Crown; Harley's advisors suggest that he obtain the patronage of a government minister—effectively selling his electoral vote for gain—in order to obtain the lease; Harley would then take any profit made from the land beyond the rent payable to the Crown.

12 *the καλον*: see *Sensus Communis, an Essay on the Freedom of Wit and Humour*, by Anthony Ashley Cooper, 3rd Earl of Shaftesbury, where in explaining the contention that 'beauty is truth', especially in reference to painting, he has a footnote beginning as follows: 'The *ready apprehension*, as the great master of arts [Aristotle] calls it in his Poetics . . . where he shows that the καλον, the beautiful or the sublime in these above-mentioned arts, is from the expression of greatness with order, that is to say, exhibiting the principal or main of what is designed in the very largest proportions of which it is capable of being viewed.' See Shaftesbury, *Characteristics of Men, Manners, Opinions, Times*, ed. Lawrence E. Klein, Cambridge Texts in the History of Philosophy (Cambridge: Cambridge University Press, 1999), 66, n. 48.

Cestus of Cytherea: the girdle of Aphrodite, which had the power of enhancing the beauty of anyone who wore it and of inspiring love in the beholder of the person wearing it (V).

13 *dialect of St. Jameses*: St James Palace, the royal residence in London; thus, courtly language.

incomparable simile of Otway's: These are the pathetic dying words of Monimia, the heroine of Otway's *The Orphan* (v. i. 415–17):

> Methought I heard a Voice,
> Sweet as the Shepherd's Pipe upon the Mountains,
> When all his little Flock's at feed before him.

See *Works*, ed. J. C. Ghosh (Oxford, 1932), ii. 82 (V).

puzzled a Turk . . . materialism: the Turk's 'principles of female materialism' (that is, that women have no souls) is apparently a myth derived from foreign travellers' deductions from the way Turkish men treated their women. For the fallacy, see Paul Rycaut's *History of the present state of the Ottoman Empire*, 4th edn. (London, 1675), 268, and Robert Walsh's commentary on the engravings of T. Allom in *Constantinople* (London, *c.*1840), i. 13; and for authoritative refutation, see E. J. Gibb, *A History of Ottoman Poetry* (London, 1900), i. 36, and T. P. Hughes, *A Dictionary of Islam* (London, 1885), s.v. 'Woman', sec. II: 'It has often been asserted by European writers that the Qu'ran teaches that women have no souls. Such, however, is not the case . . . ' (I owe these references to Miss Susan Skilliter) (V).

15 *caudle-cup*: for a medicinal drink of warm gruel, wine, and spices.

19 *He resolved . . . repulse*: Mackenzie wrote of this incident later: 'The Man of Feeling a real picture of my London adventures—Palpitation of the heart walking along the pavement of Grosvenor Square to a man of high rank to whom I had a letter of introduction, but who unlike the Baronet in *The Man of Feeling* received me with the greatest kindness . . . ' (*Anecdotes*, ed. Thompson, 190) (V).

20 *the existence of objects depends on idea*: a position most notably associated with the British empirical tradition of John Locke and George Berkeley.

    ORDINARY: 'A public meal regularly provided at a fixed price in an eating house or tavern' (*OED*).

21 *pure West-Indian*: rum punch.

22 *Butcher-row*: a street in Smithfield, near the great cattle market (V).

    match betwixt the Nailor and Tim Bucket: probably a boxing-match. Boxing had gained substantially in popularity during the mid-eighteenth century but then fell into disrepute because of the number of fixed matches. Vast sums of money could be at stake, with reports of £50,000 changing hands on a single fight; boxing is emphatically not one of the fine arts in the traditional sense of the term.

    gauger: an exciseman, and thus a lowly profession.

23 *Bedlam*: the Hospital of St Mary of Bethlehem; originally in Bishopsgate, it became a royal foundation for the care of lunatics in 1547 and moved to new buildings in Moorfields in 1675, but was infamous for its poor treatment of inmates.

24 *conjectures of Sir Isaac Newton*: Sir Isaac Newton (1642–1727) published his predictions concerning the return of comets in Volume 3 of the second and later editions of *Philosophiae Naturalis Principia Mathematica (Mathematical Principles of Natural Philosophy)*, 1713 (translated into English, 1729).

    South-sea annuities, India-stock: huge speculation in the South Sea Company in 1720 resulted in the collapse of the company and financial disaster for large numbers of investors; it became synonymous with the ephemeral nature of 'city' money as opposed to the safety of landed wealth. The East India company suffered a similar fate in the 1760s: see note to p. 76.

    a plum: 'The sum of £100,000' (*OED*).

25 *Mr. Bentley*: Richard Bentley (1662–1742), the famous editor of classical

texts, most notably of Horace; Bentley's aggressive personal and scholarly style won him a place in Swift's satirical *Battle of the Books*.

25 *From Macedonia's madman to the Swede*: from Alexander Pope's *An Essay on Man*, epistle IV, 11. 220; Pope refers to Alexander the Great and Charles XII of Sweden (1682–1718).

Chan of Tartary: the mythically wealthy and powerful fourteenth-century emperor of Cathay, known to English readers from *The Travels of Sir John Mandeville* (*c*.1500).

26 *Light be the earth on Billy's breast*: Petersen has found the source of the mad woman's quotation, which is John Gay's *The What D'ye Call It*, 2.8.1 (see *Dramatic Works of John Gay*, ed. John Fuller, Oxford, 1983, 1.199–201). As Petersen notes, the ballad, sung by the character of Kitty Carrot, is also the source for Mackenzie's madwoman (Petersen).

27 *Socratic pleasantry ... spirit of a Diogenes*: Socrates' dialogic method provides the model of conversational civility recommended by Shaftesbury and others. Diogenes, on the other hand, was the Athenian originator of Cynic philosophy, who lived in extreme poverty and despised most human aspirations and ideals (he is said to have carried a lamp through Athens in daylight 'in search of an honest man').

28 *perpetual disgust*: there is another autobiographical element here: 'I have said somewhere that the brother of the misanthrope in *The Man of Feeling* found he should never be rich but he might be very happy. That character and his disgust with his profession nearly my own case.' (*Anecdotes*, 190) (V).

29 *horn-book*: a device used in schools for teaching basic literacy. 'A leaf of paper containing the alphabet (often with the addition of the ten digits, some elements of spelling, and the Lord's Prayer) protected by a thin plate of translucent horn, and mounted on a tablet of wood with a projecting piece for a handle' (*OED*).

31 *Arthur's*: Arthur's Chocolate House was set up in 1755, when Robert Arthur moved the chocolate business from 69 St James Street (White's Chocolate House, later White's Club) to nos. 37–8. See Bryant Lillywhite, *London Coffee Houses* (London, 1963), item 54 (V).

Newmarket: a town in Cambridgeshire famous for horse-racing and part of the circuit of fashionable activities.

35 *piquet*: also picquet: 'A card-game played by two persons with a pack of 32 cards (the low cards from the two to the six being excluded) in which points are scored on various groups or combinations of cards, and on tricks' (*OED*).

38 *harts-horn drops*: ammonia, or the aqueous solution of ammonia (the chief source of which was formerly the 'horn' or antlers of a hart).

39 *CULLY*: 'A man deceived or imposed upon; as, by sharpers or a strumpet' (Johnson) (V).

40 *bubbled*: duped, cheated.

42 *circulating libraries*: borrowing libraries, mostly stocked with popular
    fiction and 'light' works, became increasingly successful in the later
    eighteenth century, and were often a target of satire because of their
    perceived ill-effects upon female readers.

48 *millenery work*: the millinery trade was often associated with prostitution.

57 *murrain*: plague or pestilence (*OED*).

58 *chay*: vulgar corruption of 'chaise', a term applied to various pleasure or
    travelling carriages (*OED*) (V).

59 *to smoke the old put*: to smoke: 'To sneer, to ridicule to the face'; put: 'A
    rustic clown' (Johnson). Eric Partridge, in his *Dictionary of Slang* (Lon-
    don, 1937), adds that *put* in this sense seems to have been slang until
    *c.*1750, colloquial until *c.*1830, and adds a second meaning—'a chap, a
    fellow'—which was generally applied contemptuously to old persons, as
    in *Vanity Fair*, Bk. 1, ch. xi (V).

    complacent: here retains its original sense: 'Civil; affable; soft' (Johnson),
    like 'complacency' below (pp. 64, 75), to which Johnson gives three
    senses: '1. Pleasure: satisfaction. 2. The cause of pleasure; joy. 3. Civility:
    softness of manners' (V).

61 *Shakespeare . . . a link-boy*: a link-boy was 'a boy employed to carry a link
    [i.e. torch] to light passengers along the streets' (*OED*).

64 *Salvator*: Salvator Rosa (1615–73), Neapolitan poet and artist especially
    famed for landscapes and battle-scenes who, with Claude Lorraine and
    Nicholas Poussin was immensely popular in the eighteenth century. See
    James Thomson's lines from *The Castle of Indolence*, 'Whate'er Lorraine
    light-touched with softening hue, | Or savage Rosa dashed, or learnèd
    Poussin drew . . . ' (I, 38). Here the person described as part of a land-
    scape 'scene' is a verbal imitation of the characteristic effect of a Salvator
    Rosa landscape. On Salvator Rosa, see Samuel Holt Monk, *The Sublime:
    A Study of Critical Theories in Eighteenth-Century England* (New York:
    Modern Language Association of America, 1935), 193–6.

65 *tell it you . . . walk*: the story of Old Edwards, which Mackenzie himself
    singled out in a letter of 24 January 1770 as his 'favourite passage', was
    extracted and published separately in four magazines between 1778 and
    1810, as well as in numerous gift-books and anthologies.

72 *prospects*: a fashionable term for views across the landscape, but also
    suggesting the social or economic aspirations of the owner; Mackenzie
    may well have had in mind Oliver Goldsmith's treatment of the same
    theme in his influential poem *The Deserted Village* (1769), in which a rich
    new landlord sweeps away an entire village and its inhabitants in order to
    create a fashionable, but empty, landscape garden.

    "And from . . . to honour him!"——: Shakespeare, *King Lear*, I. iv. 302:
    'And from her derogate body never spring | A babe to honour her!'

74 *Fashion, Bon-ton, and Virtu*: the implication of French affectation and insincerity in all three of these terms is ubiquitous. On *Virtu*, see V's note: 'A love of, or taste for, works of art or curios, a knowledge of or interest in the fine arts' (*OED*, which also quotes appositely Fielding, *Tom Jones*, Bk. XIII, ch. v: 'They may be called men of wisdom and even vertù (take heed you do not read virtue)') (V).

75 *economist*: 'One who practises economy; hence, a thrifty and effective manager of money, time, etc.' (*OED*).

dibble: 'An instrument used to make holes in the ground for seeds, bulbs, or young plants' (*OED*).

76 *An incident*: during the mid-eighteenth century India and its administration was a subject of hot debate in Britain. East India Company employees were expected to make their money through trade, and this inevitably led to wide-scale corruption; massive speculation in the East India Company also led to the 1766 collapse in stock and huge financial losses for many individuals. In the decade after Robert Clive's victory at Plassey (1757), the East India Company effectively became a territorial power in India rather than a trading company. In Britain, returning 'nabobs' were satirized on stage (see, for example, Samuel Foote's *The Nabob* (1768), which probably had Clive in mind, and Mackenzie's own much later *Lounger*, no. 17), and attacked in newspapers and in parliament. Clive brought home huge wealth and was rewarded with an Irish peerage and a knighthood, but found himself impeached in 1767 (the year in which Mackenzie began writing *The Man of Feeling*) for misusing his office for personal gain (he was acquitted in 1773). See Philip Lawson and Jim Phillips, '"Our Execrable Banditti": Perceptions of Nabobs in Mid-Eighteenth-Century Britain', *Albion*, 16 (1984), 225–41.

79 *the tidings of Ill . . . Good*: compare La Rochefoucault (as quoted by the Earl of Chesterfield), 'On trouve dans le malheur de son meilleur ami, quelque chose qui ne déplaît pas' (One finds something not displeasing in the misfortune of one's closest friend), *Maximes et réflections diverses*, ed. Jacques Truchet (Paris, 1972), 94, and *Lord Chesterfield's Letters*, ed. David Roberts (Oxford: Oxford University Press, 1992), 89–90 and 397.

Tyburn: until the 1780s Tyburn (near what is now Marble Arch) was the place of public executions in London.

barberries: also berberries; the fruit of the shrub *Berberis vulgaris*, used for preserves, sauces, and dyes.

81 *the London Merchant*: there may be a knowing reference here to George Lillo's domestic tragedy in prose, *The London Merchant, or the History of George Barnwell*, produced in 1731. (Mackenzie's adaptation of Lillo's *Fatal Curiosity* (1736) as *The Shipwreck* was first performed at Covent Garden in February 1784.)

London-bobs: probably the kind of curtsey a metropolitan lady wearing a hoop-skirt could manage: Harley's aunt sees this as an unpleasant affectation.

mushroom-gentry: mushroom as an adjective can have the sense 'resembling a mushroom in rapidity of development or growth or in brief duration of existence; upstart; ephemeral' (*OED* 6*b*), hence perhaps *nouveau-riche*.

battle of Worcester . . . Royal Oak: at the battle of Worcester in 1651 royalist forces were defeated by the parliamentary army. The legend that the future King Charles II escaped capture by hiding in an oak-tree before fleeing to France is commemorated in the name of several English pubs. All this suggests the royalist, aristocratic, and anti-'trade' sympathies of Harley's aunt.

83 *grand climacteric*: climacterics were every seven years of adult life: the grand climacteric is 'the 63rd year of life' (*OED*).

84 *'The little dogs . . . bark at me!'*: Shakespeare, *King Lear*, III. vi. 57–8.

87 *the higher part of education*: the reference to the neglect of the 'culture of the heart' is common in works on education in this period. George Turnbull, for example, appeals to the example of ancient Persia, where 'they took care to educate the heart as well as the understanding: but who thinks of the strange task at present!': *Observations upon liberal education, in all its branches* (London: A. Millar, 1742), 6.

Will smile, and smile, and be a villain: Shakespeare, *Hamlet*, I. v. 109.

93 *macaroni*: perhaps a reference to the affectation by foppish young men of foreign fashions in dress, furnishings, and manners. The term came from a society of enthusiasts for Italian culture, but the absurdity and effeminacy of many such polite males led to the term being extended to any kind of folly or excess, especially that which aped foreign manners.

100 *Decipit . . . imitabile*: Horace, *Epistles*, I. xix. 17: 'We imitate the vices of the great, mistaking them for the causes of their greatness.'

	Oriental Tales
WILLIAM BECKFORD	Vathek
JAMES BOSWELL	Boswell's Life of Johnson
FRANCES BURNEY	Camilla
	Cecilia
	Evelina
	The Wanderer
LORD CHESTERFIELD	Lord Chesterfield's Letters
JOHN CLELAND	Memoirs of a Woman of Pleasure
DANIEL DEFOE	Captain Singleton
	A Journal of the Plague Year
	Memoirs of a Cavalier
	Moll Flanders
	Robinson Crusoe
	Roxana
HENRY FIELDING	Joseph Andrews and Shamela
	A Journey from This World to the Next and The Journal of a Voyage to Lisbon
	Tom Jones
	The Adventures of David Simple
WILLIAM GODWIN	Caleb Williams
	St Leon
OLIVER GOLDSMITH	The Vicar of Wakefield
MARY HAYS	Memoirs of Emma Courtney
ELIZABETH HAYWOOD	The History of Miss Betsy Thoughtless
ELIZABETH INCHBALD	A Simple Story
SAMUEL JOHNSON	The History of Rasselas
CHARLOTTE LENNOX	The Female Quixote
MATTHEW LEWIS	The Monk

The Oxford World's Classics Website

www.worldsclassics.co.uk

- Information about new titles
- Explore the full range of Oxford World's Classics
- Links to other literary sites and the main OUP webpage
- Imaginative competitions, with bookish prizes
- Peruse *Compass*, the Oxford World's Classics magazine
- Articles by editors
- Extracts from Introductions
- A forum for discussion and feedback on the series
- Special information for teachers and lecturers

www.worldsclassics.co.uk

American Literature

British and Irish Literature

Children's Literature

Classics and Ancient Literature

Colonial Literature

Eastern Literature

European Literature

History

Medieval Literature

Oxford English Drama

Poetry

Philosophy

Politics

Religion

The Oxford Shakespeare

A complete list of Oxford Paperbacks, including Oxford World's Classics, OPUS, Past Masters, Oxford Authors, Oxford Shakespeare, Oxford Drama, and Oxford Paperback Reference, is available in the UK from the Academic Division Publicity Department, Oxford University Press, Great Clarendon Street, Oxford OX2 6DP.

In the USA, complete lists are available from the Paperbacks Marketing Manager, Oxford University Press, 198 Madison Avenue, New York, NY 10016.

Oxford Paperbacks are available from all good bookshops. In case of difficulty, customers in the UK can order direct from Oxford University Press Bookshop, Freepost, 116 High Street, Oxford OX1 4BR, enclosing full payment. Please add 10 per cent of published price for postage and packing.